JOSIE MATTHEWS'S LIST OF LOVE LESSONS:

✓ Being generous does not mean showering your woman with gifts. You must be generous with your heart and share your feelings. (Are you nervous yet?)

✓ Learn to be sentimental. Remember what she wore on your first date, not that she made you late for the department bowling championship.

✓ Hear what we mean, not what we say. (Yes, mind reading is a learned skill.)

✓ A little macho is a good thing. Women like the strong, silent type…just not too silent.

✓ Be thoughtful. Give her flowers for no reason. (That means you shouldn't expect to get lucky, then pout if you don't.)

✓ Always pick up after yourself. The shoes go in the closet, not in the middle of the living room floor.

✓ Learn to hold her in your arms and make her feel safe, even if that means you'll miss the kickoff for *Monday Night Football*.

✓ Make your woman laugh and you'll have her heart forever.

✓ The most important lesson: Whatever you do, don't fall in love with the "Love Lessons" teacher!

Dear Reader,

My, how time flies! I still remember the excitement of becoming Senior Editor for Silhouette Romance and the thrill of working with these wonderful authors and stories on a regular basis. My duties have recently changed, and I'm going to miss being privileged to read these stories before anyone else. But don't worry, I'll still be reading the published books! I don't think there's anything as reassuring, affirming and altogether delightful as curling up with a bunch of Silhouette Romance novels and dreaming the day away. So know that I'm joining you, even though Mavis Allen will have the pleasure of guiding the line now.

And for this last batch that I'm bringing to you, we've got some terrific stories! Raye Morgan is finishing up her CATCHING THE CROWN series with *Counterfeit Princess* (SR #1672), a fun tale that proves love can conquer all. And Teresa Southwick is just beginning her DESERT BRIDES trilogy about three sheiks who are challenged— and caught!—by American women. Don't miss the first story, *To Catch a Sheik* (SR #1674).

Longtime favorite authors are also back. Julianna Morris brings us *The Right Twin for Him* (SR #1676) and Doreen Roberts delivers *One Bride: Baby Included* (SR #1673). And we've got two authors new to the line—one of whom is new to writing! RITA® Award-winning author Angie Ray's newest book, *You're Marrying Her?*, is a fast-paced funny story about a woman who doesn't like her best friend's fiancée. And Patricia Mae White's first novel is about a guy who wants a little help in appealing to the right woman. Here *Practice Makes Mr. Perfect* (SR #1677).

All the best,

Mary-Theresa Hussey

Mary-Theresa Hussey
Senior Editor

Please address questions and book requests to:
Silhouette Reader Service
U.S.: 3010 Walden Ave., P.O. Box 1325, Buffalo, NY 14269
Canadian: P.O. Box 609, Fort Erie, Ont. L2A 5X3

Practice Makes
Mr. Perfect

PATRICIA MAE WHITE

SILHOUETTE *Romance* ®
Published by Silhouette Books
America's Publisher of Contemporary Romance

For Lar, the love of my life and best friend.

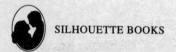 **SILHOUETTE BOOKS**

ISBN 0-373-19677-6

PRACTICE MAKES MR. PERFECT

Copyright © 2003 by Patricia Sherman White

This edition published by arrangement with Harlequin Books S.A.

® and TM are trademarks of Harlequin Books S.A., used under license.
Trademarks indicated with ® are registered in the United States Patent
and Trademark Office, the Canadian Trade Marks Office and in other
countries.

Visit Silhouette at www.eHarlequin.com

Printed in U.S.A.

PATRICIA MAE WHITE

completed her first novel at age eleven. It was a haunting suspense with a cliff-hanging phone call the reader never heard! More than twenty years later—and a bit wiser about storytelling—she rediscovered her passion for fiction, giving up her career as a public-relations specialist to write full-time. She has been nominated for RWA's prestigious Golden Heart Award, and has won several writing contests nationwide. Patricia found her very own tall, dark and handsome hero in college and they've been married for more than twenty years, proving that happily-ever-afters really do exist. The Whites live with their two sons, two dogs and two cats in "The White House" in a Chicago suburb. When she's not writing, she's usually negotiating curfews with her teenager, shuttling her younger son to and from baseball or chasing cats out of the toilet. Stop by her Web site, www.patwhitebooks.com, or write her at Patricia Mae White, 126 E. Wing St., #170, Arlington Heights, IL 60004.

Dear Reader,

I'm thrilled to be sharing my dream with you—my dream of publishing my first romance novel. My sights have been set on this goal for seven years, but it wasn't just to publish any book. My dream was to publish a book that would make you smile.

Practice Makes Mr. Perfect is a romantic comedy inspired by the differences between men and women, and the idea that what we think we want and what we really need isn't always the same thing. I thoroughly enjoyed writing this book and poking fun at how clueless men can be. Yet I believe that's what makes men and women a perfect match—our differences provide balance to our relationships.

Blessed with a wonderful husband who has kept me laughing for more than twenty years, I'm convinced that laughter is a balm to the soul. I hope that Brett and Josie's story makes you smile and forget the stresses of everyday life.

That said, I'm off to shuttle my boys to sports camp, vacuum up dog hair, feed the cats, balance the checkbook (my husband is really laughing now), empty the dishwasher, finish the seventh load of laundry, etc. Until next time…

Keep smiling!

Patricia Mae White

Chapter One

"I love you."

"Say it again."

"I love you."

"One more time."

"I love you."

"You're getting close."

"Aw, hell, this isn't going to work." Detective Brett Callahan stood and ran his hand through thick tawny hair. He paced the living room of his suburban Chicago apartment looking like a predator in search of prey.

"No, it's getting better. Really." Josie Matthews folded her legs beneath her on the leather couch.

"This whole thing is driving me crazy," he said, turning to her.

A fine-looking specimen, that one, Josie thought. Good thing they were just friends. Anything else would be way too dangerous.

"I just don't get it," he said. "I've taken her to

dinner, sent her flowers, even got Stadium Club tickets to a White Sox game.''

Oh, brother, no wonder Simone Trifarra, the woman Brett was dating, didn't take him seriously. The guy was clueless. ''Baseball will do us in every time,'' Josie said.

He narrowed his blue-green eyes at her, not appreciating her sense of humor in such dire circumstances.

''Sorry.'' She shifted under her friend's scrutiny. ''It sounds like you're doing everything by the book, so to speak.''

''Well, it's not working. If I asked Simone to marry me tomorrow, she'd say 'no.' I just don't get it.''

As he towered over her, she tried to ignore his too-broad shoulders tapering to trim hips. She didn't dare make eye contact. He had an eerie knack of reading people's minds, and if he read hers he might misinterpret her hormonal lapse for an invitation to curl up on the sofa next to her for some serious one on one.

Sure, and turtles dance. She was just Jo, his bowling partner, the girl upstairs who watered his plants when he went hunting with the boys and force-fed vitamins down his throat when he worked sixty-hour weeks while trying to start a security business on the side.

''This shouldn't be that hard,'' he said. ''We get along great. I think I love her. Why do I have such a hard time saying it?''

''It's a guy thing,'' Josie said.

He stopped and stared her down. Uh-oh. She'd been caught eyeing the way his butt filled out his snug Levi's.

''And you know this how?'' he said.

Ouch. Of course he wouldn't think it was from her

vast expertise about men. Brett and his cop friends thought of her as one of the guys.

"Thanks a lot, Callahan," she said.

"No, I mean, you're obviously not a guy," he said.

"You noticed?" In a mock primp, she fingered her short blond curls sticking out beneath her Chicago Bears cap.

"Come on, Jo. Help me out."

He sat beside her on the couch and the strong scent of male mixed with spiced aftershave tickled her nostrils.

Get a grip. This is Brett, your bowling partner, your pizza buddy.

A man in love with someone else. Thank goodness for that. One more reason to resist temptation. There's no way she'd get involved with a cop, not that she'd gotten involved with any man since she lost her husband nearly five years ago. He'd died after his equipment malfunctioned while skydiving. She'd never risk her heart again, especially to a man like Brett whose very job put him in danger.

Brett touched her shoulder and heat shot down her arm to her fingernails. And they say fingernails have no feeling. Well, just because she was celibate didn't mean she was immune.

"What?" he said.

She glanced into his eyes, her heart beating a little faster. "What, what?"

"You smiled."

"I did?"

"Women," he said, an exasperated edge to his voice. "One minute you're all over us, the next you're giving us the silent treatment because we didn't notice your new hairstyle."

"And all you can think about is work and football," she shot back.

"Hey, I like hockey," he said.

"Amazing."

"Come on, Jo. Teach me what a sophisticated woman wants. How she wants it."

Anger burned low in her belly. She'd spent five years of marriage trying to be sophisticated for Danny but always came up short.

"Why are you asking me? Do I look like an expert on the subject?" She fingered her threadbare jeans above the knee. A huge perk of working from home as a freelance copywriter was being able to wear comfortable clothes and no makeup.

"Who else can I ask?" Brett said. "I'll be the joke at work if the ladies find out I need help in the love department, and you know the guys at the police department, they're merciless. Besides, you were married once. What happened between you and that guy, anyway?"

"Wouldn't you like to know," she said.

She'd never told Brett about Danny's death because she couldn't stand people pitying her. Sure Brett knew she'd been married, but she'd never told him more than that. He was the one person in her life she knew wanted to be with her because of who she was, not because he felt sorry for her. She knew he'd pity her if he found out she'd been widowed at twenty-four. Brett always took care of people.

But she was done with relying on others to care for her. After losing Danny she realized how important it was to take care of herself.

"Come on, Jo, I need some serious one on one."

"And I need something to drink." Jumping to her

feet, she crossed the room to the kitchen of his modern apartment. She whipped open the refrigerator, welcoming the cool air. She was greeted by a white take-out container, three bottles of cheap beer and a half-eaten hunk of cheese wrapped in cellophane. How did this man survive?

She found a pewter beer stein in the cabinet and filled it with cold tap water. It was one thing to bowl with the guy, share a double-dough bacon pizza and watch *Lost in Space* reruns with him. But to teach him how to be Don Juan? This wasn't her forte. She'd been out of circulation for years and wasn't up on current dating rituals.

Heck, she'd only dated, only loved one man her whole entire life. She was no expert on seduction or snagging the mate of your dreams. After all, Danny had found her, waitressing at the Lucky Duck Pancake House in her small, rural hometown of Keller, Wisconsin.

She'd been a shy, naive girl whose biggest accomplishment was winning a blue ribbon in the Keller County pie-eating contest in the sixth grade. Even at nineteen, when Danny walked into her life, she'd only been out of the state a handful of times. There was too much work to be done on the farm for the family to take extended vacations.

She took a sip of cool liquid and considered her unexpected attraction to Brett. Must be her isolated lifestyle and landmark thirtieth birthday just around the bend. She'd thought she'd have it all by then—husband, children, happily ever after. Funny how things rarely turned out the way you'd thought.

Walking back into the living room, she stepped out

of the warpath as Brett continued his frustrated pacing.

"Relax," she said. "You've kept Miss Society on the line for what, four months now?"

"Yep. She's it. I can tell."

"Because you've broken the Callahan world record for relationships?"

"That and the burning in my gut."

"Spoken by a man who eats pepperoni pizza for breakfast, lunch and dinner."

"And I can't sleep."

"The pepperoni pleads guilty."

"And I think about her all the time."

"Of course you do. You've been celibate since you made detective a year ago, then into your life walks Miss Perfect Body." She tried to keep the envy from her voice. Some women were born models. Josie was born with hips.

"She does, doesn't she. Have a perfect body, I mean." He stopped dead in his tracks and gazed across the room as if imagining his goddess.

"Knock it off, Detective. How on earth do you nail the bad guys when you've got Simone on the brain?"

He grinned, a broad, dimpled smile. "She thinks me being a cop is sexy."

Josie shook her head at the thought of women drawn to men in dangerous careers. There were enough risks in life without looking for trouble. These women obviously hadn't a clue what mind-numbing emotional pain felt like.

"Yeah, nothing like breaking up domestic fights and teaching kids the danger of drugs to really turn a woman on," Josie said, trying to stay upbeat.

"I don't tell her about the routine stuff. Actually, I don't talk much about my job," he said.

"So, it's the badge that does her in. Tell me, do you place it above the bedpost before you make love?"

"Cheap shot, Jo. But I'll do whatever it takes to make her love me. She's perfect. Smart and sexy, well-bred and classy. Nothing like your typical woman."

"Hey, I resent that remark," she said with the right amount of indignity in her voice.

"You know what I mean."

Yep, she did. Josie had been typical once, small-town and naive. Then she'd met her Prince Charming. He'd thought her cute and perky. She'd thought him enchanting. Unfortunately, his parents considered her a gold digger, unsophisticated and not nearly good enough for their son. No matter how hard she'd tried, Josie couldn't get the love and respect she'd hoped for from her in-laws.

Regardless of what his wealthy family thought, it had been a head-on collision with love and she'd done everything in her power to make Danny happy.

"Okay, so what's the problem telling Simone how you feel?" she said, refocusing on Brett's crisis.

"Because I don't want to screw this up," he said. "Simone's the one. I've just got this feeling." He collapsed on the sofa with a grunt. "I sound like a sap."

Her heart went out to him. "No, you don't. But love isn't always simple…or easy." The words caught in her throat. *Easy* was not a word she'd use to describe her years trying to fit in as a Matthews, trying to be the cosmopolitan woman Danny needed.

"I just want the perfect wife, the perfect life. Is that so much to ask?"

She touched his shoulder, not knowing what to say. Josie hadn't expected perfect, but she'd been blessed with pretty close to it for a brief three years. How could she fault Brett for wanting to taste it himself?

Sure, there were stressful moments in Josie's marriage, times when she didn't know which fork to use on the appetizer, or which family heirloom to wear with which dress. She'd tried so hard to fit in. Danny had always assured her he'd love her no matter what. She wondered what he'd think if he saw her today, dressed in ratty blue jeans and a T-shirt, sporting a temporary tattoo of a pro-wrestler on her arm courtesy of the Sherman girls across the hall.

"Listen," she said. "If you love Simone, just tell her."

He shook his head, stood and marched to the window overlooking Arlington Towne Square.

"Brett?"

"I'm out of time, Jo. She's bringing her parents to town next week. I need to lock this up by the time they get here."

"Spoken like a true cop."

"Josie," he warned.

"Okay, okay. My best advice? Be yourself."

"I want to impress them, not scare them half to death."

An image of Brett dressed as the Grim Reaper banging on her balcony window on Halloween crossed her thoughts. Somehow she couldn't picture Simone appreciating his juvenile sense of humor.

She wondered what Simone did see in him. Was it his tenderness, which had him dressing up as Santa and visiting an inner-city homeless shelter last year? Or his compassion, when he sat up all night with his partner, Mulligan, whose girlfriend had been injured in a car accident?

She walked up beside him and touched his arm. He glanced over his shoulder. He was a good eight inches taller than Josie, and when he looked down at her, his left cheek dimpling, she couldn't help but be warmed by his smile. No matter what curve life threw him, and she suspected he'd been thrown a lot, he'd somehow remained an optimist, so boyish in some ways it charmed her to the core. Did Simone see this in her future husband?

"What's that saying about marrying the girl, not the parents?" she offered.

"At this rate I'm not marrying anyone. If I only knew how to make her love me."

She sighed, knowing only too well that you couldn't *make* anyone love you. She'd learned that lesson over and over from Danny's family.

"Just relax. Stop pressuring yourself," she said.

"You sound like my meditation teacher."

"You take meditation?"

"Quit after a week."

"Maybe that's your lesson. Patience."

He restarted his march through the living room, tunneling his hand through his hair. "I've put a lot of time into this."

"It's not a case, Brett. It's a woman."

Jo's words stopped Brett cold. Not just *a* woman, but *the* woman. A beautiful, sophisticated woman wanted Brett "the punk" Callahan from the South Side and he wasn't going to let anything prevent him from snagging this heavenly creature. She appreciated him, admired him. She was the angel that would complete his life.

Simone was supportive, loyal and classy, and classy women believed in you, stuck with you. For the duration.

He turned and considered Jo, his bud, his sci-fi movie pal. There was something charming about her even though she didn't dress fancy or wear a lot of makeup. She was short and round at the hips, wore jeans and T-shirts mostly, and tamed her unruly short blond curls with a navy blue Bears cap. Must be another bad-hair day.

Jo was his only chance.

He was sunk.

He sat on the couch, struggling against the urge to jump back up and do five more laps around his living room. Everything was in place. He'd put in his ten-plus years on the force, working overtime to earn him the detective spot, and he'd made great strides in starting his security business. He was more than ready to move on with the next step of his life. Marrying a supportive wife, having a few kids, maybe even getting himself a minivan. Surrounded by a loving family, he'd finally have the stability and happiness he'd never had as a child.

The Callahan household was more of a battleground than a loving home. His parents fought so loud over Dad's irresponsibility with money that the neighbors would call the cops. A couple of uniforms would show up, give the usual lecture and leave. Dad would be right behind them, heading to some offtrack betting dive, leaving Mom to her bottle of bourbon. On the nights when Dad didn't come home she'd take out her anger on her kids, verbally berating them to tears. Brett hated seeing his little sister cry, so he learned how to protect her by taking the brunt of the abuse.

"Brett?" Josie snapped her fingers to get his attention.

"Yeah, well, Simone's flying in a week from next Tuesday from Boston with her parents to check things in the Chicago office," he said. "I've got to figure this thing out by then."

Jo sat down at the opposite end of the sofa. "What do you think this 'thing' is, exactly?"

"Why I can't say those three words to her, for one. Hell, I can say them to you."

"But you don't mean it. Maybe the thought of saying it to someone you really love is scaring the pants off of you."

Now, that was ludicrous. He'd waited his whole life for someone to say it to. "I'm not scared of anything."

"Then I guess you don't need me." She started to get up.

He lunged across the sofa and grabbed her wrist, surprised by the softness of her skin. Okay, so maybe he was scared. The thought of getting so close to his dream and watching it pass him by terrified him.

"Don't go," he said.

"The first step is admitting you're scared."

"You make it sound like I belong in a support group."

She laughed, a light, feminine sound so contrary to her tomboyish looks. Jo always surprised him when he least expected it. Like the time he caught her singing while working on her compact station wagon. It was a young, soft sound, so unlike the expert who wielded the wrench.

"Who knows, maybe I can find you a support group on the Internet," she said.

"See, that's another reason why you're the perfect person to help me with this." He released her wrist and she settled on the arm of the sofa. Good, he hadn't chased her away. "You're a whiz at research." She'd told him she'd learned to research and write tight copy during college, while waitressing to pay tuition.

"Somehow I don't think hydraulic-brake maintenance for eighteen-wheelers is going to help you."

"But you can research articles on making a woman fall in love or how to make me into the perfect guy. Come on, Jo. Please?"

Studying her odd expression, he realized he was holding his breath. Damn, he couldn't believe she was actually making him beg for help. The last time he'd begged was when he was eleven and his father had broken into his baseball bank for money to bet on the horses. Brett had been saving up for his first ten-speed bike. Instead he got a black eye from the old man. Yet the physical pain didn't come close to the humiliation of begging. Never again.

He sat straight and ran his palms down his jeans. "Forget it. I just thought...you were married once so you know what works."

"But my experience is definitely dated."

"Once a woman, always a woman."

"True enough," she said. "And you picked yourself a fine one indeed."

"How would you know? You've never met Simone."

"I've been in the hallway after she's left your apartment. Expensive perfume tends to linger."

"She only wants the best," he said, honored that a classy woman like that would be attracted to him.

"Then why's she dating you?"

He grabbed the morning paper, still rolled up in blue plastic, and swatted Josie on the shoulder.

"Hey!" She swung her arms in defense and the cap tumbled off her blond waves. "See, that's another reason why I won't help you. You'll retaliate if you fail."

"Not true. But it's a dumb idea. I should have figured this wasn't your thing."

And it wasn't. Jo was a great gal, always there when he needed her to feed the fish or bring in the paper because he'd been working a case three days straight. She bowled more strikes than Butch or Mulligan and could rattle off Bears statistics from 1985.

Yet Brett sensed a vulnerability about her that reminded him of his kid sister. Growing up, Brett protected Lacy from the ugliness of the Callahan household.

Sometimes he found himself wanting to protect Jo, from what he wasn't sure. She'd made it clear on more than one occasion that she didn't need or want his help, and sometimes that hurt. Oh, well, old habits die hard.

He touched her hand. "So, you'll help me?"

She shrugged and went into the kitchen again for another drink. "Bring me something while you're in there," he said.

She poked her head around the corner, thumbing her hair behind her ear. "Water or cheap beer?"

"I'll have you know Mulligan brought that over for poker night last week."

"Sure he did." She smiled and disappeared into the kitchen.

"Wise guy. I'll ask him to help me. He's got all kinds of books on the art of seduction."

"Tell you what," she said, peering around the corner. "I'll give you a free love lesson." Her eyes twinkled with mischief. "Don't confuse love with sex. To a woman they're not necessarily the same thing."

"Yeah, thanks for nothin'."

She chuckled and disappeared again.

Whose fool-brained idea was it to ask Jo for help, anyway? She was one of the guys, not a femme fatale.

Still, he thought about that last shot: *Don't confuse love with sex.* The words spun around in his head like a slot machine about to land on three cherries. And spun, and spun. Nope. No jackpot.

Nervous energy made him bolt from the sofa. He walked to the makeshift office in the dining room and fingered the list of prospective clients Simone had given him. She'd encouraged his business venture, even knowing the kind of stress it would put on a relationship. With these leads he'd be well on his way to having his security business up and running within the year.

He stilled at the thought of abandoning the Arlington PD. Police work had become everything to him, his identity, the ultimate proof that he could be something more than the son of an unemployed factory worker with a gambling problem, and an alcoholic mom. Okay, so maybe money problems drove mom to the bottle. But that didn't excuse her lack of parenting.

To think Brett had nearly ended up in juvenile hall thanks to the anger eating away at him. A good thing Officer Johnson came along, locked him up and gave him the lecture of a lifetime. Brett changed his tune, got himself a good part-time job and practically raised his kid sister. He'd never end up broke and bitter like his parents, another reason running his own business was so appealing.

Yet, as a cop, he had to admit he liked the occasional on-the-job rush of adrenaline when a drunk wanted to take off his head with a bar stool, or when he'd been assigned to stake out a suspected drug dealer and busted him.

Quitting hadn't been his original goal. Starting up Callahan Security was about proving himself a successful entrepreneur and being financially secure. Being better than his old man, tougher and stronger.

But there was more to life than money. There was the love of a good woman, something he'd never had. Sure, he'd dated. He'd even taken a few females out more than once. But casual dating and snagging Ms. Right were two different things.

Glancing into the dining room mirror, he rubbed his face with his hand. He wasn't such a bad-looking guy if you ignored a twice-broken nose and a few battle scars from street fights as a kid. Simone didn't seem to have a problem with his looks. There had to be something else that kept her at arm's length.

"It's just three words," he muttered. "I...love... you."

"Oh, you narcissistic devil," Jo said, coming toward him with a pewter mug in one hand and a Fraternal Order of Police mug in the other. She shoved the FOP mug at him. "You'd better not let Simone know how you feel about yourself."

His retort was cut off by the ringing phone. He grabbed the receiver. "Yo!"

"Yo? What kind of greeting is that?" Simone's crisp, professionally trained voice said.

He gripped the phone tighter. "Simone?"

"Most human beings say 'hello' or 'hi' or—"

"Hey, gorgeous."

"Better. How's my hero-cop doing?"

"I'm not a hero, Simone."

Josie rolled her eyes and headed for the door.

"Wait, we're not done," he said to her.

"Who's not done?" Simone asked.

"Oh, just my neighbor. No one important."

Jo stuck out her tongue.

He mouthed, "Help me."

"Don't sell yourself short, Detective," Simone said. "Daddy says you are what you think you are. If you think 'hero,' you'll be a hero."

Her voice did him in every time. The clear enunciation of every syllable rang across the fiber-optic wires and zapped him straight in the heart.

"I'm just a cop, Simone, no big deal."

"A cop, soon-to-be-entrepreneur, just like Daddy. He started with a handful of change and a milk crate. Now he's a millionaire. That could be you someday."

"Simone," he protested, yet he liked how much she believed in him.

"Hang on, my other line's ringing." She put him on hold.

He placed his hand over the receiver. "I'm going to say it, Jo. I'm going to tell Simone I love her."

"Over the phone?"

"It's good practice."

"Ten bucks says you can't," she challenged.

"You're on."

Simone clicked back on the line. "Sorry."

"Listen, Simone, I have to tell you something."

"Tell me in person when you see me Sunday."

"Sunday? This Sunday?" His gut dropped to his knees. He couldn't possibly be ready so soon. To meet her father, to ask for her hand in marriage, to say "I love you."

"We're coming in early. Isn't that great?" she said.

"Yeah, great." Now he had less than six days to perfect himself.

"Daddy can't wait to meet you."

"Me, neither."

Jo got in his face and rubbed her forefinger against her thumb, then sailed out the front door.

"Hey!" he called.

"Hey, what?" Simone said.

"Nothing, sorry."

"Only six more days," she said. "Think of me tonight when you slip under those satin sheets I bought for your birthday."

He didn't have the heart to tell her he hadn't tried them out yet. Brett was a flannel kind of guy.

"Daddy's just going to love you," she said. "Hang on, someone just walked in." The sounds of seventies pop music filled the line.

Six days. Only six days. Impossible. But then, he'd faced impossible odds before, like getting out of that run-down neighborhood and dragging his little sister with him.

A bang at the door interrupted his misery. Probably

Jo back to taunt him. Then again, maybe she'd decided to help. He was actually hopeful.

He whipped open the door and was greeted by a short, roundish man, chewing on an unlit cigar. ''Got a delivery for Jo Matthews.''

''Upstairs,'' Brett directed.

''Not home.'' He shoved the signature board at him.

Not home? More like the guy didn't want to make the climb.

''Fine.'' Brett signed his name and took the box.

''I'm back,'' Simone said.

This was it, his chance to say the words that would bring him and Simone closer, prove to her he was a guy worth hanging on to…for life.

''Simone, I—''

''I've got to run. Until Sunday, hero-cop.''

''Right, Sunday.''

The line went dead.

He banged his forehead against the wall. He shouldn't have tried saying it over the phone, anyway.

Deep down he knew it wasn't just those three words that would make Simone agree to be his wife. He had to transform himself into the ultimate romantic, a sensitive male who cherished his woman, spoiled her and said all the right things.

The hoops a guy had to jump through for true love.

His gaze drifted to Jo's package. The return address label read ''Nadine's Naughty Necessities: The Ultimate Store for Lovers. A Gift from Your Secret Admirer.''

His fingers itched to rip open the strapping tape and discover what, exactly, a man was sending Jo.

He needed help, fast, and Jo was the closest thing

he had to an expert. She just got a box of naughty goodies from a secret admirer. That gal was full of surprises.

"I'll bribe her to help me." He'd pick up a few bags of Oreos, a twelve-pack of red pens for editing her articles and maybe a new sports cap. Then he'd march up to Jo's place and demand she transform him into the perfect man. Nicely demand. He knew when you pushed Jo hard she pushed back harder.

Time was running out and Brett was desperate. She had to help him win over Simone. After all, what were friends for?

Chapter Two

"I will not write for some kinky sex catalog," Josie protested to her friend, Wendy Banks, over the telephone. She leaned back in her swivel chair and glanced at her home office calendar.

"It will be a good experience. I sent you some freebies to help you write better copy," Wendy said, chuckling. "Who knows? Maybe you'll shed that chastity belt and go have some fun for a change."

"I have fun," Josie defended.

"Cloistered up in that apartment like a hermit?"

"Hey, I get out. I go bowling on Fridays, and do bingo on Sunday nights at Our Lady of Perpetual Sin."

"Bingo?" Wendy scoffed. "They're probably all old enough to be your grandparents."

"Not true. Father Paul is only thirty-seven."

"Great, the only person under forty and he's celibate."

"I won fifty bucks last week."

"Praise the Lord. You need a man. A *man*. A *man!*"

Josie stretched the receiver away from her ear and waited for Wendy to quiet down. She could be obnoxiously bossy, but she was also a good friend who'd put up with more than her share of Josie's dark moods.

"Why am I talking to you?" Josie said.

"Because I'm your best friend. And I got you a new client."

"Yeah, perverts."

"Don't be judgmental. Nadine's in a bind. They need copy in a week and they're willing to pay big time."

She glanced at the copy she'd just filed with the National Truck Association. The truth was she didn't have any pressing deadlines.

"So, how're things?" Wendy said. "Anything new and exciting or is that a dumb question for Miss Goody Two-shoes."

Josie sat up straight. "I had an interesting proposition today. My downstairs neighbor asked me to teach him how to make a woman fall in love with him."

"Now we're talking. I didn't know you two were dating."

"We're not. He's in love with somebody else," Josie explained.

"And he wants you to give him lessons in love? Kinky."

"Yeah, well, I feel sorry for him."

"This is that cop we're talking about, right? Tall, handsome, magnetic eyes, and a body that's perfect for the cover of *Muscle Digest* magazine?"

"That's him." And that's exactly why she'd discouraged anything other than a brief introduction between Wendy and Brett. Wendy loved men, any and all kinds. Josie couldn't risk her friendship with Brett when Wendy chewed him up and spit him out.

"Sounds like you and the cop are gonna have fun," Wendy said.

"I said no."

"Why? At least you'd get good sex out of it."

"I'm not into casual sex," Jo said. She couldn't tell Wendy that Danny had been her one and only lover. She'd never understand.

"Give Brett my number," Wendy purred.

"I don't think so. A wild woman like you would ruin the poor guy."

"At least I date. The only men you talk to are for interviews about trucks or blood-born pathogens."

"Cut me some slack. It's been a while. I'm rusty."

"All the more reason for you to take Brett up on his offer."

"He's a good friend. I want to keep it that way."

"Then let me have him."

"Forget it."

"He'll be forever grateful."

"I'm hanging up now."

"I'll handle him with kid gloves, I swear," Wendy said as Josie hung up the phone.

She pushed away from her desk and walked into the living room, stretching her arms above her head. As she ambled toward the kitchen, she righted a sloppy stack of magazines on the coffee table. A headline caught her eye: Making Your Man Beg for More.

That gave her an idea. She'd pick up a few magazines featuring articles on unraveling the mysteries of a woman. She shoved aside the guilt at not wanting to help Brett with some personal instruction. But she was no expert in the physicalities of love, and the thought of touching Brett, kissing him—whoa, baby. How'd she end up down this road again?

She opened the fridge and welcomed the blast of cold air. She grabbed a blueberry yogurt, snatched a box of animal crackers from the counter and went to the living room. Maybe she should give him Wendy's number. If anyone knew what a woman wanted, it was Wendy.

She settled on the thick-cushioned sofa and let out a sigh. Wendy could pass along a few prized secrets for Brett to use on Simone. After all, there was no way on earth Josie would risk revealing her limited knowledge of seduction.

Limited being the key word. She'd met the one and only love of her life when she was nineteen. Danny had always been the leader in their relationship, gently guiding his naive wife to new and exciting places, both in bed and out.

At times Josie had tried to be the seductive type. But growing up with four brothers taught her the value of being tough, not the skills of being sexy. She could throw a touchdown pass as good as Jake, Pete, Chris or Adam and she was damn proud of it. Too bad her older brothers still saw her as the baby they needed to protect. Occasionally she got that same feeling from Brett, which irked her no end. She'd worked hard to become a tough cookie, an independent woman able to take care of herself. A woman who no longer spent hours on her makeup and nails, stressing over which dress to wear to one special event or another.

Helping Brett woo Simone was not a job for Josie. It felt all wrong.

Yet deep down, in the pit of her stomach, it felt exciting, risky and more than a bit naughty. Another reason not to do it. She didn't want to screw up the best relationship she'd had in years. Her unexpected friendship with Brett was a true gift.

She'd cut herself off from her family after Danny's death. Her parents and big brothers had smothered her with their concern.

Poor Josie, a widow at twenty-four. Poor Josie, now what will she do? She's lost everything.

And she had. She'd even lost herself. That epiphany was devastating. Josie needed to stand on her own for once, all by herself.

She dipped a cracker in her yogurt, then popped it into her mouth. Why did Brett have to go to these lengths? A woman would be crazy not to fall for the guy. Although if Josie was shopping for a man, Brett wouldn't make her A list, the list reserved for stable, non-risk-taking men, the kind you could count on coming home at night.

Obviously Brett's job was more of a turn-on than a deterrent for the ever-perfect Simone, the goddess with the long hair, even longer legs and flawless skin.

Josie glanced at her bare toes, decorated with purple, green and pink nail polish, another result of the recent visit from the girls across the hall. That was the best perk of working from home. She could write in her sweats, her underwear or nothing at all. No one was the wiser, except Fred, her pet iguana, and he wasn't going to tell anyone.

Dunking another cracker, she punched the remote control. She scanned all sixty-four channels until she landed on an animal program featuring the mating rituals of Australian lizards.

"Hey, Fred. Check it out," she called over her shoulder. Fred stared straight ahead in his usual statuesque pose.

They'd just gotten to the good part when someone pounded at her door.

"Hang on!" She got up and shook the crumbs off her hands over the plastic yogurt container.

The door vibrated with another bang.

"Okay, okay! I'm not deaf." She whipped open the door and found herself eye to eye with a brown box.

"Surprise!" Brett shoved the box at her and crossed the threshold.

"You shouldn't have."

"I didn't. I intercepted. But I did pick up some pens and Oreos while I was out. They're on top."

She eyed him, wondering what he was up to.

"Don't look at me like that." He breezed past her and planted himself on the couch. "Blueberry and animals."

He dipped a cracker into the yogurt and chomped away.

"Make yourself at home," she said.

He was already engrossed in the television program. "Hey, did Fred see this?"

"Yep." She placed the box on the kitchen counter and studied it, dying to know the contents of Wendy's bribe. She didn't dare open it in front of Brett.

"What's in the box?" he said.

"Later." She ran her fingers across the address label. It read Nadine's Naughty Necessities: The Ultimate Store for Lovers. Too bad she didn't have anyone in her life to try it out on.

"I wanna see." His words, whispered by her ear, shot goose bumps across her shoulders. She didn't know he'd come up from behind her.

"Get out of here. It's girl stuff."

"I like girl stuff."

"Go away." She elbowed him in the ribs. He didn't flinch.

He placed his arm around her shoulder, so casual, so friendly, as if she was his little sister.

"This admirer of yours got a name?" he said. "I'll do a background check when I get into work."

"You most certainly will not." Sheesh, when was he going to get it through his thick skull that she didn't need a protector?

"Why, has he got a record?"

"I can take care of myself, thank you."

"So you've said." He didn't look convinced. "Still, you don't know who this guy is."

"Trust me, I know."

"Yeah?"

"Yeah."

"Huh. I never pegged you as being into—" he eyed the box "—naughty stuff."

No, he probably thought her into mundane sexual encounters with the lights off. The truth panged her heart.

"The things you don't know about me would curl your toes," she said.

"Yeah?" He smiled.

The disbelief in his voice stirred something wicked inside her belly. She could be a knockout if she put her mind to it. She just hadn't had a reason in a very long time.

She snatched a knife from the butcher block and aimed dead center at the package. The flaps broke free and she dug her hands into a mound of foam peanuts. Her fingers wrapped around something soft and furry.

"Voila." She pulled out a feathered contraption.

"Since when is asking a woman to dust romantic?" he said.

"Wait a minute, there's more." Digging deeper, she wrapped her fingers around a metal tin and ceremoniously pulled it out, sending a flurry of peanuts tumbling onto the counter.

"What is that?" he asked.

"Honey-flavored body dust."

He stared at her, a confused crease to his brow.

"For your body. Get it? You dust it on your partner…" she prompted, hoping she didn't have to demonstrate. Her pulse quickened at the thought.

"O-o-o-oh." His eyes lit up, his face reddened.

"You're blushing," she said.

"I can't help it. It's like talking about the birds and the bees with your kid sister."

A pit knotted in her stomach. Why? It wasn't as if she wanted a man's attention, ever. She knew both the wonders and pitfalls of falling in love and had promised herself it would never happen again. She'd never find herself alone and desperate because she'd become so dependent on a man who was taken away from her.

Danny had been so tender and charismatic. And he loved *her!* Little Josie Denton from Keller, Wisconsin. She'd tried her best to be the wife he needed. She was cheerful and accommodating and followed his advice when planning her days. She'd become so dependent on him that when he died she found herself with nothing. No husband, no future and no sense of who she was anymore.

"What else have you got in here?" Brett sunk his large hands into the box and pulled out a transparent red negligee. He held it up to his chest and burst out laughing.

"*You* are going to wear *this?*"

She gritted her teeth and wished for once she was six inches taller and ten pounds lighter around the hips. Damn him for thinking it absurd that a man would find her desirable. Her feminine pride wounded, she snatched the negligee from his hands.

"Actually, it won't stay on long. But it was romantic of him to send it, don't you think?" She said the words out of irritation more than anything. There was no secret admirer, no man to send her sensual gifts or flowers.

For a fleeting moment, she wanted one. Not a serious partnership. She'd sworn off those for good. Yet the idea of an admirer doting on her warmed a chilled corner of her heart.

"Wait, there's more," he said, digging clumsy fingers into the sea of white foam packing. He plucked a pair of skimpy panties from the box.

"Nice. Fire-engine red." He squinted to read the tag. "Whaddya know. Cherry-flavored." He held them to his nose and sniffed.

"Get your nose away from my panties." She snatched them from his hand and shoved the items back into the box. His rich, deep laughter echoed through the apartment as she marched the package to the bedroom and placed it on her antique dresser.

"Sorry, Jo. I just never pictured you as, I don't know, wearing that kind of stuff," he called out.

Of course he didn't. She was dependable Jo, not Sexy Simone. She went back into the living room and plopped onto the sofa, reaching for her yogurt. He sat next to her and tipped up the bill of her hat.

"Do you ever take this off?" he said.

"Only when my secret admirer and I go out." She shot him a blazing grin, then focused on the television.

"Jo, I really need you," he said, his voice deeper than usual.

She stilled, slowly turning to study his pleading, aquamarine eyes. Did she hear him right? He *needed* her?

"You do?" Was that hope or fear tickling her belly?

"You have to help me with Simone," he said.

She breathed a sigh of…relief. Yes, that's what it was. She didn't want anything other than friendship from Brett.

"She's coming back early," he said. "You can help me. I know you can. You know what a woman wants. I had no idea women were into stuff like body dust."

He placed one arm around her shoulder and pulled her against him. She started to make some snide comment but the words stuck in her throat. Her gaze caught on his perfectly shaped lips. All it would take is a slight lean forward and she could have her sample. What could it hurt? She'd bet anything he tasted all male with a hint of goofy grape, his favorite bubble gum.

He cocked his head to one side. "Jo?"

Her gaze drifted up to his eyes, tinged with confusion.

She jumped to her feet, accidentally dumping the half-eaten yogurt into his lap.

"Hey!"

"Sorry, hang on, I'll get something to clean it up." She raced to the kitchen and grabbed some paper towels. This was twice in one day she'd lusted after her friend. What the heck was the matter with her? One thing for sure, she couldn't be trusted. She grabbed a notepad and scribbled Wendy's number. It was the least she could do.

"I've got something for you." She walked into the living room and handed him the number.

"What's this?"

"My friend's phone number."

Brett fingered the piece of paper, trying to make out the scribbles, so unlike Jo's impeccable handwriting. He started to ask the pronunciation of the girl's name, Wiley, Willy, when something rubbed against his crotch.

"What the—"

"I've ruined your favorite jeans," she said, swiping a wet paper towel across his crotch. "Soak them in really cold water when you get home. Try club soda. I've got some if you need it."

"Ah, Jo?"

"You'll like Wendy," she said, continuing to dab at his jeans. "She's a lot of fun and pretty, in a Lucille Ball kind of way. But I'll warn you, she's a handful."

Any second now he was going to totally embarrass himself with his body's automatic response to female hands on him. No, he couldn't be reacting to Jo's touch. He just didn't see her that way. Then again, it had been too long since he'd made love to a woman. Work had kept him too damned busy.

He pushed her hand away. "Stop. Okay? I'm fine."

"But your jeans." She started toward him again.

"This is going to get embarrassing in a minute."

She froze, her gaze drifting to his crotch. A flush of pink crept up her neck to her cheeks. Full, round cheeks that reminded him of Dee Dee Sellers, a girl he had a crush on in the fourth grade.

She shoved the paper towel at him, cleared her throat and took a step back. "I...um..." She shoved her hands into her pockets. "I was trying to get the stain out, I mean...um..."

"No big deal." He shot her a reassuring smile. He'd seen her at her worst, like when Fred contracted some strange virus, and when her computer crashed last spring. She'd nearly lost all of her fairy tales that no one knew she wrote but Brett. Yet their sexuality was one topic they'd never touched.

Clearly embarrassed, she backed into an oak book-case, then turned to adjust a hardcover that was slightly out of place. Leave it to Jo to organize her way out of an awkward situation.

"Tell me about this Wiley person," he said, to ease the tension.

"Wendy." She turned to address him and her cheeks were back to their normal peaches-and-cream color. "Wendy's an art director for a local ad agency. She's a lot of fun."

"I'm not interested in fun. I need a love tutor."

"She'll be great. She dates a lot and was engaged once, or twice." She grabbed the cordless phone and punched a number. "You can talk to her right now."

"But—"

"Hi, Wen. Remember that cop friend I told you about?" Jo said into the receiver.

Brett got up and walked into the kitchen. Wadding the paper towel into a ball, he sailed it into the garbage can. He didn't know this Wendy person from Adam, and it bothered him that Jo wouldn't agree to help. What was her problem? Was she that repulsed by him that she couldn't teach him a few tricks with a little hands-on instruction?

Heading back into the living room, he eyed her crazy outfit: threadbare jeans and a T-shirt that read Truckers Do It on the Road. She'd traded her baseball cap for a psychedelic headband holding back waves of blond hair. He smiled to himself, admitting he'd have a devil of a time learning the finer points of love from Jo without bursting into laughter.

He'd laughed before at the idea of her wearing that negligee and thought he might have hurt her feelings. Maybe it was a good thing Jo's friend was willing to help. The last person on earth he'd want to hurt was Jo.

They had a special relationship—as comfortable as hanging out with a guy, yet more intimate. Wrong word. *Intimate* wasn't something Brett did easily, if ever. Years of being belittled cured him of opening up.

He shifted onto a bar stool and Jo shoved the phone at him with a wicked grin. "Here."

He didn't want to talk to Wiley or Wendy or whatever her name was. Frustration burned hot in his chest and he hadn't a clue why. Gripping the receiver, he took a deep breath. The lengths he had to go for true love.

"Hello?" he said.

"Hey, handsome. I hear you need some one on one."

He cringed at the inference. The idea wasn't to cheat on Simone. That's why a little help from Jo would have been perfect. Flirting with Jo was definitely not cheating.

"I could use a few pointers, yeah," he admitted.

"Pick me up tonight. Eight o'clock. Josie's got the address."

"Where are we going?"

"You'll see. Bye-bye...lover."

The line went dead. What had Jo gotten him into?

He shoved the phone at her. "Call her back and tell her I've changed my mind."

She stared him down. "I will not."

"Where's that piece of paper? I'll call her." He fumbled in his pocket, searching for the woman's number.

She swiped the phone from his hand. "What's the matter with you? You need a teacher. I got you a teacher."

"I don't like her voice."

She eyed him. "You're scared? Of a pretend date?"

"I'm not scared. I just didn't want to do this with a stranger."

She pulled him off the bar stool and aimed him toward the door.

"I've done my part, buster. I set you up with an experienced teacher in the art of romance. In less than a week you'll be able to make Simone say 'I do.' Now, go home and get ready for your big date."

"Jo?" He turned to her.

"What?"

"Thanks, I think."

"Sure. Anything else I can do for you?" she said, her voice dripping with sarcasm.

"Actually, there is one thing. The kitchen drain's clogged again," he said. "I was going to fix it tonight but—"

"I'll take care of it while you're out. I've got your spare key in the cookie jar. I'll expect my usual payment."

"A bag of Oreos?"

"Make it two," she said.

"Rates have gone up."

"Inflation. Have fun tonight, loverboy."

She shut the door and he stood there, staring at the peephole for a good minute. There'd been an edge to her voice, an irritation, and he couldn't read her eyes. That was a first.

He headed downstairs, thinking that maybe he shouldn't have asked her to fix the drain. It probably seemed like one favor too many, considering she'd just hooked him up with her girlfriend.

Or maybe it was one more thing for her to do tonight. Did she have a date with her secret admirer? Damn, he wished she'd let him do a background check on the guy.

Would her admirer take her to dinner or stop by and ask her to model her new sexy underwear? He could see it now…Jo, wearing her Bears cap, the red negligee and multicolored toenail polish. He chuckled to himself and started down the stairs to his apartment.

Another image flashed across his thoughts. But this time Jo wore the cap…and nothing else. He flew down the stairs, his breathing more labored than usual.

"Out of shape," he muttered, opening the door to his place. He had three hours to get his head together and be ready to learn. He just hoped this Wendy person was the expert who could teach him.

Josie swung the wrench, the sound of metal hitting metal piercing her eardrums. "I'm gonna win, you crusty, rotten piece of no good missile-flocker."

Wedged under Brett's kitchen sink, she adjusted the red bandanna on her head and eyed her enemy. This pipe would be the end of her self-control.

"I will prevail!"

Scrunching up her legs to shimmy herself into a better position, she shoved the wrench around the pipe ring. She clenched her teeth and gave it a twist. It didn't budge.

"Argh!" She swung at it again, hoping sheer frustration would jar it loose. Instead a stream of water squirted her in the face. "I hate you!" she cried, releasing her pent-up frustration.

She'd been cranky ever since Brett stopped by to ask for Wendy's address. He looked like he'd just walked off the cover of *Cowboy Digest* in his black jeans, denim shirt and cowboy boots. Dangerous. That's the first thought that came to mind. She just hoped Wendy could handle him. For all his insecurities about love, Josie suspected he had a passionate streak that could blast a woman's self-control to pieces.

She squinted to see through the stream of water, grateful that Brett wasn't around to witness her verbal explosion. He always teased her about her self-control and addiction to order. What would he think of her now?

She gave the fitting one more shove and felt it move. Victory! The pipe came loose, shooting water and various decomposing foods into the bucket she'd placed beneath the trap. The powerful surge also splattered gray muck across her chest.

"The price just went up to three bags of Oreos!" she cried, scooting out from under the sink. She eyed the front of her T-shirt, the stench something between stale beer and dirty socks.

"This is disgusting." She stripped off the shirt and put it in his bathroom sink to soak. Then she headed for his bedroom and opened the top drawer of his walnut dresser.

"Let's see if I can ruin a shirt of yours, big guy."

As she rustled through his array of undershirts, his scent drifted up from the cotton. She closed her eyes, bringing a handful of undershirts to her face. Clean and fresh…and all male.

"I'm really losing it," she muttered, shoving the white cotton shirts back in place and checking the second drawer for a suitable T-shirt. Instead she found treasures: baseball cards, old coins, folded-up notepaper, and a plastic badge that read Junior Police Officer. She ran a finger across it. Brett always knew what he wanted, even as a kid.

She placed the badge in the drawer and her gaze caught on a small jewelry box. She cracked open the velvet box and her breath caught at the sight of a white-gold ring with five small diamonds lined across the top. It was handsome and classic. She chewed at her lower lip. Unable to resist, she slipped it on her finger and stretched out her arm to admire the multi-faceted stones as they sparkled with life.

"Wow," she whispered. "Simone is one lucky woman." She imagined Brett slipping the ring on Simone's finger, gently, with that dimpled smile of his. Yet something didn't fit. Brett seemed too down to earth for Simone, too real.

Then other memories flooded to the surface: Danny's tender proposal; his mother's disapproving scowl; the hectic wedding reception; the awkward wedding night.

Oh, how she wished she could have been the refined woman Danny needed. She'd tried so hard, hosting coffee get-togethers and joining fund-raising committees, reading books on etiquette and practicing speaking in front of a mirror. In less than a year Josie could work a room with the best of them. Yet deep down she always felt like little Josie, the country girl.

The front door opened with a crash, bringing her back to earth. She glanced into the mirror, horrified at her reflection. Her lace bra was the only thing between her and total nakedness from the waist up. She pulled the plug of his bedroom lamp, plunging herself into complete darkness. She tried to slip the ring off, but it clung to her finger like leg irons on a prisoner. Voices drifted from the living room.

"I don't remember leaving the lights on," Brett said. "Jo?"

Now what? She couldn't let him walk in on her half naked. She dove into the closet and tugged repeatedly at her finger. Her knuckle swelled in protest.

How was she going to explain this? Rifling through his personal things. Getting his fiancée's ring stuck on her finger.

"Bedroom's this way," Brett's voice echoed.

"If you're sure you're up to this," Wendy answered.

Josie strained to hear more. What the heck was going on? She fumbled for a shirt; stiff polyester greeted her fingers. Great. The only thing hanging there was police blues.

"Please be gentle," Wendy said as they entered the bedroom.

Good God, what were they planning to do? Josie held her breath.

"Do you want me to do this or not?" Was that Brett's angry voice? Had Josie misjudged him that much?

A tumble, crash and thud was followed by a female cry and male grunt. "Dammit. Just get on the bed."

Josie groped through his belongings for a weapon but came up empty-handed. What kind of cop didn't keep a spare billy club in his closet? She picked up a hard-soled shoe, the shine of patent leather slick beneath her fingers. It would have to do.

Josie pressed her ear to the door.

"Enough, already! It hurts," Wendy said.

"Then stop moving around so much." Brett sounded like a savage.

Josie sprung from the closet. "Leave her alone or I'll—" Her jaw dropped at the sight of Wendy and Brett sitting on the edge of his bed, her thumb pressed between his fingers, a tweezer in his other hand.

He looked up and blinked through his magnifying reading glasses. "Jo? What are you doing in my closet?"

Chapter Three

"Yeah, Josie, what are you doing in the closet?" Wendy repeated.

"And why are you wearing my uniform?" Brett said.

"And what's with the shoe?" Wendy added.

"I was, I thought…it sounded like you were in trouble," she said to Wendy.

"Me? I've got a splinter." Wendy cocked a brow and looked from Josie to Brett, then back to Josie. Her lips formed into a half smile. "If anyone's in trouble it's this handsome hunk of a man."

In a swift move, Wendy straddled Brett and pushed him back onto the bed. His head thumped against the wall, hard.

"Hey! I don't think—"

"I don't want you thinking, sugar." She took off his glasses and aimed a kiss for his lips. He turned away from her and she missed her mark, but he didn't. He glared at Jo, his eyes blazing fire, his hand massaging the back of his head.

"Wendy, I asked you to help him, not attack him. What kind of lesson is this?"

"The bedroom lesson," she purred, ripping open his shirt. She ran flattened palms across his chest. Josie's pulse rate jumped.

"No offense, but this wasn't what I had in mind," Brett said with polite irritation.

"Oh, right. You want to know what really turns a woman on?" Wendy took his hand and ran it across her cheek. "Hmm. That's nice."

Josie stared in disbelief. "Wendy!"

"Or maybe this." With professionally manicured nails, Wendy guided his hand down her neck, then the base of her throat, then lower still.

Something snapped inside Josie. She grabbed a pillow and started swinging. Feathers flew. Wendy shrieked. Brett grunted as Wendy pushed off of him.

Call it anger or jealousy or just plain frustration. Wendy had no right to manhandle Jo's best friend against his will.

"Okay, okay, already. I'm just kidding around." Wendy reached up to defeather her hair.

"I'm not laughing and neither is Brett." Josie stood between them, the deflated pillow clutched between her fingers.

"I've got an early appointment, anyway. Bye, Brett. It's been—" Wendy winked at Josie "—interesting, to say the least."

Josie escorted her friend to the door.

"Did you get the goodies from Nadine's Naughty Necessities?" Wendy said.

"Don't talk to me about doing you any favors. I ask you to help a friend and look how he ends up."

They both glanced into the bedroom. Brett sat up, giving them a nice view of his square, broad shoulders.

"Edible," Wendy said.

"What's gotten into you?"

"Just doing my good deed for the day." Wendy smiled.

"By forcing yourself on my best friend?"

"I wasn't talking about him. I was talking about you." Wendy shot Josie that crooked smirk. "You like the guy and I just proved it. You're jealous. That's why you came after me with the pillow."

"Don't be ridiculous."

"Josie, it's been five years. You're allowed to have a life."

"I like my life just the way it is. Uncomplicated."

"Boring."

"Go home." She shoved Wendy out the door and double-locked it. "Good deed, my eye."

Guilt, anger, embarrassment. Josie drowned in them all as she walked into the bedroom.

"Sorry about that," she said.

"Could you toss me a T-shirt?" he asked. "She ripped the buttons off this one." He fingered the denim shirt where it fell open in front.

She'd seen him shirtless before, but never paid much attention. But now, for some reason, she couldn't tear her gaze from his hard pecs and firm tummy dusted with light brown hair. *Snap out of it.*

"A shirt, right." Digging into the top drawer of his dresser, she froze at the sight of the diamond chips sparkling on her left hand. Could this night get any worse? She tugged at it one more time. No dice. She twisted the diamonds to the inside of her hand. Maybe he wouldn't notice.

She found a black T-shirt and started toward Brett, hesitating as she approached. Last month he'd hidden crickets in her bathroom when she'd stolen his parking spot. What revenge would he seek after tonight's fiasco?

"I feel bad about all this." She searched his eyes as she handed him the shirt.

He didn't look at her.

"You're really mad at me," she said.

"I'm tired and frustrated." He rubbed the back of his head where it had connected with the wall.

No doubt about it, Josie had it coming. She cringed at the thought.

"I'll just finish with the kitchen sink," she said, figuring she'd fix this one for free.

He grabbed her wrist. "Take off the shirt first."

"This shirt?" She held out her arms, the cuffs dangling below her fingertips.

"That's for police officers, Jo. No one else."

"But I ruined mine."

"Then grab a T-shirt."

She started for the dresser.

"After you hang that back up."

So, this was her punishment. Complete and utter embarrassment. He was used to sexy women. Tall, lean and alluring women were his choice picks. But Josie, she was just...well, just Josie. A whiz with a pipe wrench, a flop in the passion department.

Turning away from him, she started unbuttoning the shirt. She should just whip the darn thing off and be done with it. But the thought of him comparing her to Simone's well-toned body made her fingers tremble. How degrading to be compared to perfection.

But this didn't feel degrading. As her thumb pressed the top button through its hole, her heartbeat quickened. Was he still watching her? She slid the second button through its hole, then the third, exposing the cleavage between her breasts. Heat rose in her cheeks as the shirt came open in front. She felt his eyes roam her back as he watched her, waiting for her to turn around. Or was that her imagination?

One thing she didn't expect: how erotic it felt to strip in front of him.

Erotic?

She blinked into the mirror at her own, wanton reflection. Maybe Wendy was right. Maybe she did need a man.

But not Brett.

"You hang it up," she said. "Your pipes started all this."

Getting a hold of her senses, she took off the shirt and tossed it at his face in sudden modesty. But it didn't matter. He was staring at something fascinating on the carpet. Wonderful. Not only had she stripped in front of him, but she'd been a fool to think she'd turned him on.

She found a Fraternal Order of Police T-shirt in his drawer and slipped it on. Tying it at the waist, she headed back to the kitchen. She'd be safe there, away from him, away from the awkward moment she'd created during her little striptease.

"Oh, brother," she scolded herself.

She crawled under the sink, ground her teeth and twisted the pipe ring snugly in place. After Danny's death she didn't get close to many people. The loss had been too great, the pain too severe to chance opening up again.

Then came Brett, her lighthearted neighbor who had a way of joking her out of a bad mood and making her laugh at herself.

Josie didn't want to help Brett woo Simone because she feared losing him as a friend. But once he married Simone she'd lose him, anyway.

"Selfish creep," she muttered.

She closed her eyes. How could she call him selfish? He'd given of himself repeatedly during their two-year friendship. Like the time he'd picked her up near the Wisconsin border when her car died, or when he'd consoled her over Fred's mysterious orange-spotted condition that the vet didn't know how to treat.

He cared about her the way a best friend should care: without judgment, self-motivation or expectation. Shouldn't she do the same?

"Anything I can do?" The sound of his deep voice startled her and she bumped her head against the bottom of the sink.

"Yeeoow!" she cried.

"You okay?"

"Bumped my head."

"Good. Now we're even."

"Just run the water, will ya?" she said, trying to keep the irritation from her voice.

Water trickled through the pipes. No leakage. Her job was done. She took a deep breath and curled her fingers into the engagement ring stuck on her finger.

He treated her like a best friend. Didn't he deserve the same treatment?

"You okay down there?" he said.

"Yep." She planted the soles of her purple sneakers against the linoleum and scooted out from under the sink. "Drain's fixed. But we've got a bigger problem."

She stuck her hand out and his eyes widened.

"Gran's ring?" He gripped her hand and gently turned it this way and that.

"It was an accident. I was looking for a shirt and I noticed the box, and I'm usually not nosy, but I couldn't help—"

"You tried on Gran's ring?"

"It was so beautiful I had to get a better look. But I tried it on and couldn't get it off. Then you guys came in, and I hid in the closet because I wasn't dressed and—"

He burst into laughter and stumbled back against the counter.

"How can you laugh about this?"

"What else can I do? I'm a fourteen-year veteran of the force and I find myself pinned to my own bed, after you jump out of the closet like a banshee swinging my black patent leather shoe. What was that about, anyway?"

"It sounded like, never mind."

"You thought I was forcing myself on her?"

"No, yes, I don't know." Josie studied her fingernails.

"You know me better than that," he said.

Silence filled the room.

"You're right," she said. "I'm sorry. I don't know what got into me." Actually, she didn't dare analyze herself for fear of what she'd find.

"Dinner was a bust and now Gran's ring is on the wrong woman's finger," he said. "This has been one helluva night." He closed his eyes and rubbed the back of his head.

"Go sit down. I'll get ice for your head," she said.

"I don't need ice."

"Come on, it will ease my conscience."

"Whatever." Brett ambled into the living room and collapsed on the sofa. What a night, and all because he wanted Simone to love him.

Maybe expecting another woman to help him with his romance skills was a stupid idea. Hell, if he didn't have it, he just didn't have it. He shouldn't be surprised. It's not like his parents "had it." The only love they showed was the love of hurting each other. They were experts at that. To think a couple who supposedly loved each other could be so nasty and cruel. He'd seen how they'd suffered and decided he was never going to live like that.

That's why he needed Simone. He balled his hand into a fist and drummed it against his thigh. He wanted her to say "I do" more than anything. She was the brass ring, the dream he'd been waiting for his whole life. He'd worked hard earning a living, building respect, not having much time for romance, but he'd hoped that would come later.

"Here," Josie said, walking toward him. "Lean forward."

"I'm fine."

"Do it." She held the ice, wrapped in a towel, to the back of his head.

She had a surprisingly gentle touch.

"Your sink was a mess," she said. "You owe me four bags of Oreos."

He jerked his head to look at her. "After what you got me into tonight!"

She tipped his head down and reapplied the ice. "Okay, three."

"One."

"Two."

"Deal."

"And a six-pack of root beer for dunking," she said.

"That's disgusting."

She massaged his shoulder with her free hand. His favorite spot. Relaxation washed over him and his neck muscles loosened a bit. His mind wandered…the embarrassing moment at dinner when Wendy licked his knuckles…the crazy scene in the bedroom when Jo jumped out of the closet wielding his shoe like a machete…the heat in her eyes when she stripped off his shirt.

The bump on his head must have knocked something loose from his brain. Jo wasn't into that kind of stuff. He had to keep his eyes glued to the carpet to keep from watching her and getting turned on. Jerk. She was his friend, not a one-night stand.

"I'm sorry about the ring." Her fingers performed magic on his knotted shoulder muscles. He wished she'd stay here all night.

"You're mad, aren't you," she said. Her hands stilled and he glanced up into her apologetic eyes.

"Gran's ring really won't come off?"

"No." She extended her hand to study the jewel. "It's so beautiful. Simone's very lucky."

Her expression touched his heart.

"I hope Simone likes it as much as you do."

"I'm sure she will. Listen, I've done enough damage tonight. I'd better go." She placed the ice pack in his hand and headed for the door. "I'm sorry, again, about everything."

He stood and discreetly grabbed his handcuffs from the table. "What's the hurry? Got a hot date with your secret admirer?"

She shot him a smile that could light up the state of Texas. He took that as a yes.

Tough. The guy would have to wait until Brett was done with Jo.

He came up behind her. "You'd better cancel."

"Why?"

"Because, unless he likes dining behind bars, he's going solo tonight."

"What are you talking about?" She pulled open the door and crossed the threshold.

He grabbed her wrist and snapped on a handcuff. "Josie Matthews, you're under arrest."

"For what?" She tugged at her hand. He held tight to the other cuff, deciding if he should put it on himself, or cuff her to a piece of furniture. Somehow being handcuffed to Josie didn't feel right.

"Theft."

She stared at the ring. Her jaw dropped open. "You can't do this."

"I just did. You've got two choices—come back inside and help me out with this love stuff, or sit in a cell."

"You are such a jerk." She marched into his apartment and headed for the bathroom. "I'll get this darned ring off if my finger comes off with it." She slammed the bathroom door.

Brett laughed as he considered the measly supplies he kept in his bathroom. After all, he did most of his showering at the gym after his morning workout.

He heard a crash and a squeal.

"You okay in there?" he called.

"Like you care!" she shouted through the door.

"But Jo, I do care. I don't want to see you wither away behind bars, or in my bathroom."

She had to know he was kidding, right? Payback for the night's humiliating experience of being pinned, pawed at and nearly eaten for dessert? Actually, it felt good to have the upper hand for a change since Jo rarely let him have it.

He smiled to himself and settled on the couch, adjusting a few pillows so he could recline comfortably. This was perfect. Jo would smooth him out around the edges and by Monday he'd be picking out china patterns with Simone. By working with Jo, he wouldn't have to worry about being attacked by some wild woman, or having his intentions misinterpreted. Jo knew he needed her research and instructional skills, nothing more. Nor was she interested in anything more than friendship. He sensed her fear every so often and read the pain in her amber eyes.

She was as strong as steel on the outside, but fragile as glass on the inside. He sensed she'd never let anyone close enough to hurt her again.

He often wondered what happened between Jo and her husband. She'd only said it didn't work. Instinct told him there was much more to it, but she wasn't talking.

Could he blame her? He didn't exactly spill his guts to the woman he considered his best friend.

He glanced at the bathroom door. She was working awfully hard to get that ring off. The thought of helping him must be horrifying for her. Or was it the memory of being married?

"Damn." He sat up, thinking maybe he shouldn't have involved Jo in all this. The whole love thing could be too painful for her. Why didn't he think of that before?

The bathroom door opened and she marched toward him.

"Listen, Jo, I was just kidding. Forget I asked for your help, okay?" He handed her the key to the handcuffs. She uncuffed her wrist and tossed the cuffs at him.

"What? Suddenly I'm not good enough for you?" she said.

"No, I mean—"

"Let's get started."

"You'll help me?" he said.

"I have no choice. You'll lock me up."

"You know I'm kidding."

"Forget it. You always get your way in the end."

"If that were the case I'd be planning a wedding by now."

"Ha! I'm liking Simone more and more," she said.

"Enough with the insults. Teach me something I can use on her."

She narrowed her eyes and fingered the silver heart locket she wore around her neck. "I need paper. Lots of it. Pencils, erasers, tape and trail mix."

"Trail mix?"

"I think better when I crunch."

He got up and gathered all the supplies but the trail mix. Being a chili dog kind of guy, trail mix wasn't in his vocabulary, much less his kitchen. He fumbled around the top shelf of a cabinet and pulled out a box of peanut brittle. So it was six months old. It would be that much crunchier, right?

"No trail mix. How about stale peanut brittle?" He balanced the supplies in his arms and went into the living room. She wasn't there.

"Jo?"

"In here," she called from the bedroom.

He followed the sound of her voice and spotted her curled up on the floor in the corner.

"What are you doing in here?" he said.

"Bring me the supplies and go lie down."

"Excuse me?"

"Do you want my help or not?" She motioned for the supplies with her fingers.

"Okay, okay. Don't get bossy."

He dropped the brittle, paper and pens in her lap and stretched out on the bed. He interlaced his hands behind his head and the light went off.

"What the—" He sat up on his elbows.

"Lie down. I work better in the dark."

"Oh. I get it."

But he didn't get any of this. He wanted surefire ways to charm his girlfriend into marriage. Instead, Jo sat in the dark and he lay on the bed. Was she hoping he'd fall asleep so she could sneak out?

"How can you see over there in the dark?" he said.

"Full moon tonight."

The moonlight streamed through the window. Too bad he couldn't romance Simone under its beauty.

"Tonight I learn. Tomorrow you learn," she said. "I need to know everything about you and Simone from how you met, to who's usually on top."

"What!"

"Okay, okay, maybe position isn't necessary, but I need to know the rest—where you took her on your first date, her favorite food, things you do to make her feel special.''

He studied her, dwarfed in his T-shirt, wearing a red bandanna. She looked more like a high school kid than a woman of experience.

''Let's start with how you met,'' she said.

''Her car was vandalized. She was amazing. In complete control even though her things had been messed with. There was this air of class about her, real quality.''

He glanced at his teacher. Jo kept scribbling.

''They towed the car and I gave her a ride to her place. I couldn't believe it when she asked me in.''

His thoughts drifted to that night. He was so nervous but tried to act cool. He'd been with other women, sure. But Simone was different. She was smart and classy and...just like Mrs. Tenderlin, the woman whose hedges he'd trimmed when he was fifteen.

He'd never forget the Tenderlins, the wealthy couple he'd watched from afar. They'd shared such love, such compassion with each other as Mrs. Tenderlin kissed her husband goodbye in the morning. It was then Brett realized a classy woman was the key to happiness.

''Brett?''

''Sorry, got sidetracked. Simone asked me about work, why I joined the force. It had been so long since I'd been with a woman, I thought I was imagining her coming on to me.''

''Was she?'' Josie said, bringing him back to earth.

''I guess. She touched me a few times. Man, my heart pounded out of my chest. Like something crazy was about to happen.''

"Did it?"

"No. But she called me at work the next day and said she wanted to go out for drinks."

"What does she drink?"

"Wine, I guess."

"You guess? Brett, you have to pay attention to what your lover drinks, what she eats, what books she reads. This kind of stuff will help you clue in to what she's really about."

"I know what she's about. She's classy, smart, sophisticated, perfect."

"I never thought rose-colored glasses looked good on you, Detective. Let's get back to what you know about her."

"She's smart."

"Said that."

"She's beautiful," he said.

"Said that, too."

"She's determined."

"I'm talking specifics," Josie said. "What does she do for fun? What's her favorite song? If she could go anyplace in the world on vacation where would it be?"

"She *can* go anyplace in the world. She's rich."

"What's her favorite flower?"

"I, uh—"

"Does she like to dance? Go to movies?"

"I think she likes movies."

"You have to know this stuff. You have to prove you're her soul mate, that you can anticipate her every need, her every desire. What have you been doing these past four months—no, don't answer that."

"We went to the opera."

"Wow. I'm impressed."

"I fell asleep."

"You didn't!" She chuckled.

"I couldn't help it. I'd just pulled a twelve-hour shift followed by two hours of paperwork. Simone's dad gave her the tickets and she was so excited about going that I couldn't say no."

"So, she likes opera." More scribbling.

"Actually, she seemed more interested in who was sitting where and with whom. She kept poking me in the ribs and pointing out local celebrities."

"Must have been hell on your nap time," Jo said.

"Yeah, well, that wasn't one of my better days. I made it up to her when I took her to the ballet and stayed awake for the whole show."

"No kidding?" she said, awe filling her voice.

Familiar shame pinched his gut. A punk like Callahan appreciating the ballet? A loser like Callahan snagging a beauty like Simone? Yeah, right.

"How did the physical part of your relationship progress?" she asked.

"Do you really need to know that?"

"If you want me to help." She glanced at her notes and crunched another piece of brittle.

"Simone's the cautious type. She controls things."

"Things?"

"Yeah, like kissing…and stuff." He wanted it to end there.

"She seems happy with…stuff?"

"I don't ask her to fill out a survey and leave it on the nightstand."

"My, aren't we testy."

He rolled off the bed and paced to the window. Leave it to Jo to zero in on the real problem. "I don't want to talk about this anymore."

"This is how I do my research. I find out everything about the subject, round it out with details, then write the story. I'm approaching you and Simone the same way. I can't help unless I know it all."

"You know enough," he said, his chest tight. "Just teach me what to do to make her love me."

"What makes you think she doesn't love you?"

"She's never said it, for one."

"Have you?" she said.

"That's irrelevant."

"I'd say it's very relevant. You expect her to bare her heart and soul, but you keep yours locked up?"

"I thought women liked saying it."

"And men don't?"

"They don't use words," he said.

"Here we go again. Sex doesn't necessarily mean love."

"Good, then maybe she does love me."

"What's that supposed to mean?"

"Never mind." He studied the parking lot below, his chest tightening into a knot.

Inner voices taunted him for thinking a woman like Simone could love a low-class punk like him. He'd spent most of his adolescence in trouble, charged with disorderlies and vandalism. The rage practically drove him into a cell at Joliet.

Out of the corner of his eye he spied Jo walk across the room. Hell, he didn't want this. Didn't want her feeling sorry for him.

She touched his arm. "Brett?"

The warmth of her touch melted his resolve. He closed his eyes.

"I've been with women before," he said. "But this one…"

"What about this one?"

He took a deep breath and prepared to open his soul. "It's been four months and we haven't…" He looked into her eyes. "Why won't she make love to me, Jo?"

Chapter Four

Crunching brittle, Josie bit her tongue at Brett's intimate confession. She slapped her hand to her mouth and squeaked.

"Gee, thanks for the understanding," Brett said, glancing outside.

She put out her hand. "Ah bit ma ton," she mumbled through the stars dancing before her eyes.

"Sorry, never learned pig Latin."

"Tongue, I bit my tongue," she clarified. Blinking twice, her eyes refocused on Brett. His lost expression touched her heart.

"I haven't had brittle in a long time," she said, recovering. "It takes a certain talent to chew it safely."

Just like it takes a certain talent not to get too involved in a man's life as he shares every intimate detail, every fear and vulnerability.

She thought she could do it, truly. Then he brought up the subject of lovemaking, or lack thereof, and she lost it. This went from Jo helping out her buddy, to Jo imagining him in the throes of passion, stroking and touching his lover in the most intimate of places.

Giving. That's the kind of lover Brett would be. She instinctively knew it and couldn't get that image out of her mind. A naked Brett stretched out in bed, firm pecs, gentling hands. Giving, gentle, intense.

She cleared her throat. "I'm going to get some ice-water."

Heading toward the kitchen, she scolded herself for yet another meltdown. This was Brett, not some…some what? She hadn't let herself be drawn to another man since Danny's death.

The loss had been unbearable. It had felt like someone had cut off a part of her body, like she was half a person wandering aimlessly, looking for that missing piece. A feeling she vowed never to experience again.

Then came the realization that not only had she lost her husband in the skydiving accident, but she'd lost herself, as well. She'd depended on Danny so much, for everything. She'd never allow herself to depend on someone like that again.

She'd grown up with overprotective brothers, all four of them experts at giving her unwanted advice. When she'd married Danny she'd thought she'd broken free of that control. Instead she went from overpowering brothers to a subtly controlling husband. Oh, he wasn't bossy. He just knew how to take care of things. And she let him.

After he died she discovered how inept she was at taking care of herself, and that had to change. The last place she wanted to go was back home to become dependent all over again. Sure, her family meant well.

They loved her and she loved them. But it was time she took care of herself.

It took years to grow into an independent woman who could change the oil in a car as well as any man. She wouldn't sacrifice her independence and wholeness for anything.

Which is why she'd kept men at arm's length. Why bother getting to know them? It's not like she'd risk that kind of pain again. She also suspected love was a once in a lifetime deal. Danny was her one and only, her champion, her rock.

She heard the television go on in the living room.

Brett. Her friend, her new rock.

No. She would never depend on a man again, never give herself completely until she couldn't define where she ended and he began.

She'd certainly never get close to a man like Brett, whose very job required him to face danger head-on. Danny had a safe job in his family's real estate business, and look where he ended up: dead before his twenty-fifth birthday. There was no explanation for the equipment failure. It just happened. Brett, on the other hand, didn't just happen to walk into danger when he'd pull over a drunk driver, or help Rolling Hills' police with undercover work. He embraced danger with open arms.

Brett could be nothing more than a bowling partner, jogging pal, someone to eat her leftover pizza with.

She poured a glass of lemonade from a carton in his fridge. He must have gone shopping since this afternoon. No doubt preparing for Wendy's visit.

She shuddered at the memory of her friend's behavior and her insinuation that Josie wanted more from Brett than friendship. Well, she was wrong. As his good friend, there was only one thing to do: make it up to him. Josie would transform him into the perfect man, teach him what women liked and how they liked it. Even if it drove her insane. Someone should be happy and in love.

"You need something?" she called from the kitchen.

"Beer would be great."

She grabbed a can of beer and walked into the living room. He was stretched out in his favorite spot, the beat-up leather recliner. The remote dangled from his fingertips.

"Here." She handed him the beer. Melancholy dimmed the playfulness usually sparkling in his blue-green eyes. She couldn't stand to see him like this, this big, strong, fun-loving guy haunted by his own fears.

"I really did bite my tongue," she explained, sitting on the couch, inches away from him.

"Interesting choice of words."

"Stop being so paranoid."

"It's a guy thing. We have this mild fear of rejection, in bed, out of bed, but especially in bed. Your reaction just made it worse." He flipped to a Super Bowl rerun from years ago.

"Do you want me to help you or not?" she said.

"I guess."

"Then turn that off." She reached for the remote.

"Not on your life," he said, shoving it between his thigh and the arm of the recliner. "It's the Bears-Patriots game. We win for a change."

"And you've seen that game how many times now?"

"I stopped counting at ten."

"Then turn it off." She leaned across him, digging for the remote.

"Forget it," he protested, grabbing her by the shoulders.

A gentle grab for such a big man. Gentle, kind, funny. She still puzzled over Simone's reticence. Heck, if Josie was an emotionally healthy woman in the market...

But she wasn't, and this wasn't about her. It was about Brett snagging the woman of his dreams.

"Do you or do you not want to win over Simone, body and soul?" she said, her face so close that his scent seeped into her skin. She had to admit she'd miss this guy when he rode off into the sunset with Miss High Society.

"I do," he said.

"See, you're learning already. You can say the two magic words." She swallowed hard, trying to lasso her wits and remember what they were talking about. Oh, right, love lessons. "You're a quick learner and I'm an excellent teacher. Together we can do anything."

He chuckled. "I almost believe you."

"Almost?"

"Forget it, Jo. It was a bad idea." He shifted her to the arm of the couch. His hands lingered on her hips and she struggled to remember the last time she'd felt such warmth, such stability from a man's hands. It had been a long time. It would probably be forever.

"You're not giving up that easily," she said.

He flipped on the television and turned up the volume. Josie studied her friend, a mixture of playful child and wounded adult. It meant so much to him to finally live the perfect life with the perfect wife.

She just hoped it was everything he expected once he got his dream.

"Remember lesson one?" She snatched the remote from his hand and turned off the television.

"Give me that," he said.

"Lesson one, what is it?"

"Quit while you're ahead." He reached for the remote and she shoved it under her bottom.

"You think I won't try to get that?" He narrowed his eyes.

Her body lit with anticipation at the thought of Brett wrestling her for the remote.

"First of all, don't confuse love with sex," she said.

"Then why do they call it making love?"

"Lecture first, questions later." She grabbed her legal pad from the table and made a slash across the top. "Let's forget this making love thing and focus for a minute on making you into the perfect man."

"A minute? You're an optimist."

"Positive thinking, Detective. Let's talk about what women like in general. They like men who are sentimental, compassionate, generous, smart, funny, maybe even a little macho, and that's just the tip of the iceberg. I'll expand on those basic themes."

"I'm a dead man." He leaned back in the chair and closed his eyes.

"Knock it off." She whacked him with the legal pad. "Let's start with lesson one—Sentimental." She wrote the word on the top of the page.

"Can't we start with the easy ones? Like macho?"

He puffed out his chest. "I broke Mulligan's nose last month at a department basketball game."

"You didn't!"

"Okay, so it was an accident. But it sounds macho."

"We're starting with Sentimental. Let's hear about the first day you and Simone met."

"June 13."

"I'm impressed."

"It was also the day I beat Mulligan by twenty points in one-on-one basketball. A big day for me."

Josie shook her head. "What was she wearing?"

"Uh...blue, no, red. No, she hates red. Says it's for streetwalkers. Wait a minute, it's coming." He pressed his forefinger and thumb to the bridge of his nose. "Orange, that's it. But not really orange. It was like this orange-brown thing, with a flowered scarf, well, not flowers, exactly."

"Old age must be wearing down your memory."

"Bull." He stared her down. "Mickey Mouse nightshirt, red socks and yellow slippers."

"That's what she was wearing?" Josie said, shocked.

"That's what you were wearing the first time I saw you running through the hallway with shredded lettuce clutched between your fingers."

"Ack. Don't remind me." She looked away, wanting to forget the embarrassing day Fred had escaped and Brett had moved in.

"Almost asked for my deposit back," he said. "I thought, 'That's why the place was so cheap. It's overrun with loony teenagers.'"

"Teenagers?"

"Yeah, you." He smiled.

Her heart sank. Silly girl, why feel bad about him seeing you as a teenager? You surely don't want him to be attracted to you as a woman.

"Gotta admit that wasn't one of my better days," she said.

"I don't know. I figured if they let someone like you live here, then I'd fit right in."

She smiled, she couldn't help herself. He had fit in, from the beginning, with Dora, the retired ballet dancer, and with Katy Sherman and her two girls.

"Let's get back to our lessons," she said. "I'll type out a lesson plan. We've got what, six days?"

"If I'm lucky."

"You'd better take some time off work," she said.

He shook his head. "No way."

"You'll have to take time off to devote to your partner."

"Mulligan?"

"Your life partner, not your work partner, ding-dong."

"Nah. Simone likes that I work so much. She says I'm ambitious, like her dad."

"Trust me, when the chips are down, she'll want your undivided attention, to know that she comes first. She'll expect you to take time off at the snap of her fingers."

"She wouldn't do that." His eyes widened with panic.

"In any event, we need time to perfect you over the course of the next six days," she said.

"I'm on days. Shouldn't be a problem. We can do our thing all night."

We can do our thing all night. Her pulse rate shot up at the inference. Blasted hormones. Maybe it was time to circulate again, find a willing and able man to satisfy her physical needs.

"All night long is out of the question," she said. "My bedtime's eight."

"You're pathetic."

Not really, she just liked her nightly ritual of taking a candlelight bath while listening to the sounds of Yanni.

"Let's get back to the list—lesson one—Sentimental."

"Should I be taking notes?" he said.

"I'll type this out in triplicate." She looked at him and smiled. "Just in case you lose your copy."

"Are you calling me disorganized?" he said.

"Did you or did you not lose your remote for two weeks?"

"Ten days, and too much TV is a bad thing."

"Pay attention. Lesson two—Compassionate. Three—Generous," she scribbled, chewing intently on spearmint gum.

Brett watched her in fascination. She was one determined woman. Determined to help him win over the woman of his dreams. But what would Josie get out of the deal?

When this was over he'd have to do something nice for her, really nice. He'd take her to J. B. Lechner's farm out in Crystal Lake. His friend owed him a favor. He'd take time off and make a day of it. Hell, he had enough comp time to take off a month. They wouldn't miss him for one day.

A special, well-deserved day for his buddy Jo. The smell of hay, countryside and damp earth always relaxed him and brought him peace. Maybe it would remind Jo of her life back home in a quiet farm community up north. He often wondered why she'd moved away.

"Lesson seven—"

"Seven? We've only got six days," he protested.

"We'll double up. We need to cover all the bases. Seven." She narrowed her eyes at him in challenge. "Hear what we mean, not what we say."

"You teach mind reading?"

"A little intuition goes a long way. Should be a no-brainer for a guy who relies on intuition for work."

"Being able to tell whether someone was really peering through Mrs. Zatski's living room window or whether she needs someone to talk to is one thing. Knowing when a woman wants the opposite of what she says—that's impossible."

"Not impossible, a learned skill. Lesson eight," she continued.

Overwhelmed, he sat back and watched her chew at her lower lip as she dreamed up more hoops for him to jump through, more torture. Hell, he wanted to be the perfect guy. Was he that far off?

Dumb question. It had taken him thirty-plus years to finally attract a woman of quality and breeding, a woman who would make his life complete. Sure, a few women had come before. But they didn't have the qualities to make a perfect life, namely class and breeding, devotion and loyalty. Just like Mrs. Tenderlin.

Brett's parents said rich people were conceited and self-centered, thought themselves too good for the world. The Callahan family line. Money was always key, or lack of money in his family's case. They never had enough and never let him forget it. Nor did they ever let him forget where he came from, that he'd always be just like them: angry, bitter, struggling to make ends meet.

As a teenager cutting lawns for All Affordable Landscaping, he'd learned just the opposite. Brett would lean against an aging oak tree in the wee hours of the morning and watch Mrs. Tenderlin wrap her arms around her husband's neck and kiss him goodbye. It was a long and sweet kiss, passionate and desperate.

Brett shouldn't have watched but couldn't help himself. Mrs. Tenderlin was a vision of an angel, dressed in white, her strawberry-blond hair pulled back into some kind of knot, a few wisps dancing across her shoulders. Mr. and Mrs. Tenderlin held each other for a good ten seconds before the guy tore himself away and hopped into his Jaguar. Brett would watch him drive off, a broad smile on his face, and imagine what it felt like to be loved and cherished so completely.

His father had never experienced that feeling, nor had his mom. Dottie and John Callahan were masters at bitter words and hateful games. As Brett got older he became a master of escape, begging All Affordable for work so he'd have an excuse to stay away.

Week after week Brett would watch the Tenderlins and ache for something he never thought to have. He ached for love, support and devotion from a life mate.

Someone like Mrs. Tenderlin.

No one else would bring the fine qualities to a relationship that made a partnership work. The very qualities lacking in his parents' marriage.

He glanced at Jo, who wrote furiously on her notepad. She was amazing when she set her mind to something, like last year when she volunteered to bring hot meals to the homeless sleeping on lower Wacker Drive. He argued that it was dangerous, that if those people needed food they'd find a shelter nearby. But Jo had seen some local TV special about the homeless not leaving their spots for fear they'd lose their makeshift homes.

He'd driven her compact station wagon while she'd handed out home-cooked meals. When he'd asked her why she didn't go home for the holiday she'd evaded the question. When he pressed harder for an answer, she looked him straight in the eye and asked why he didn't go home to visit his parents. He'd dropped the subject. Revealing his background, his dysfunctional family, was not something he could do, ever.

"Ten..." she said.

Hells bells. He would have to take time off to fit in all his lessons.

"What more could you possibly have on that list?" He got up, sat next to her on the couch and glanced over her shoulder. She scooted away. Did she find him that unappealing that she didn't want his shoulder rubbing up against hers? It shouldn't matter, but it did.

"Come on, let me see." He leaned closer, the scent of her hair tickling his nose. It was a sweet scent, like sun-ripened raspberries.

"Trust me, big guy. By the time we're through you'll have Simone eating out of the palm of your hand." She turned and winked, her smile lighting up her mischievous eyes.

He smiled back, appreciating her confidence and enjoying her teasing nature.

"You remind me of my kid sister, Lacy," he said.

"Gee, thanks."

"I meant it as a compliment."

"Lesson one…" she began.

Barely listening, he wondered if she was, in fact, someone's little sister. She held her cards damn close, especially when it came to her childhood, family and marriage.

He'd respected her wishes but often wondered what would drive a man away from a warmhearted girl like Jo. She was fun to be around, witty and had a heart of gold.

Too bad she wasn't right for Brett.

"Let's start with both Sentimental and Compassionate," she said. "Think of things you did together. Bring them up in the course of conversation, naturally, don't force it. Compassion means listening to her and really feeling her feelings."

He must have shot her a stupefied look.

She readjusted herself on the couch. "Try to put yourself in her shoes, understand how she feels. Don't dismiss her as a rambling female."

"How did you—"

"Mulligan's voice carries. Last week in the hallway I heard him call his girlfriend a rambling female. Being sensitive means trying to understand Simone's pressures and challenges. Offer help where you can. Hold her in your arms and make her feel safe."

"This is how I usually hold her." He reached out and wrapped his arms around Jo, pulling her close. She squeaked.

"I'm not hurting you, am I?" He loosened his grip.

"You just surprised me," she mumbled into his shoulder.

He held on for another few seconds, trying to imagine Simone in his arms, leaning into him so completely.

Instead Jo's wild hair tickled his lips and her fingers balled the cotton of his shirt above his heart. She was a great teacher, all right. He couldn't remember ever sitting like this with Simone for any length of time. Theirs was a frantic courtship filled with social commitments and discussions about his security business.

Jo nuzzled his chest as he stroked her shoulder. She made it look so easy. The holding, stroking, just being. He could sit for hours like this, maybe even days or…years.

Whoa! Wrong woman, Callahan.

"Uh, Jo?" he whispered.

No answer.

He glanced down into the face of pure contentment, eyes closed, lips curled into a slight smile. Obviously, she was comfortable, too. A strange feeling tangled his gut into a knot.

"Jo!"

"Huh?" She jumped to her feet, knocking over her empty glass of lemonade and scattering papers to the floor. "Sorry."

"You fell asleep?" he said, stunned that she could be so relaxed she'd fall asleep in the middle of a conversation.

"Sleep, me? No, well, what time is it?" She glanced at her watch. "Sheesh! It's nearly ten. What did you expect?" She dropped to one knee and plucked papers from the floor. "I'll organize this mess tomorrow and get you a typewritten report."

"Did I pass?" he joked.

She glanced up, confusion creasing her brow. "Huh?"

"Just now, on the couch, being compassionate and all that. How did I do?"

Her gaze drifted to where she'd been sitting, then back to him. "Great, wonderful, fabulous. Passed with flying colors," she rambled, then stood, papers hanging from her arms. "Good job, lesson one mastered."

"You sure?"

"Sure, sure. An A plus. Gotta go." She raced for the door.

"Jo?"

She hesitated, hand on the doorknob, not turning around. "Yeah?"

He wanted to ask if he'd really done okay. If she thought there was hope for him.

"Never mind," he said.

"You did great, Brett." She opened the door and disappeared into the hallway.

Somehow, he didn't believe her.

Chapter Five

She had the entire next day to get her wits back, thank goodness. That scene last night was embarrassing, to say the least. What on earth had gotten into her, falling asleep in Brett's arms like that?

Leaning back in her office chair, she fiddled with Simone's engagement ring on her finger and studied the computer screen. The list nearly complete, she could see where she had her work cut out for her. After all, how was she going to teach Brett the perfect way to touch a woman when she wasn't sure herself?

She'd been a naive girl when she'd fallen for Danny. A part of her regretted not being able to bring more to the marriage in the physical sense. But he'd never complained.

It was Josie who couldn't shake the feeling that she didn't live up to the physicality part of their relationship. Guilt flooded her thoughts. Danny had loved her, faults and all. That's what had counted most.

In the meantime, she needed to focus on helping

Brett. Taking a sip of lukewarm coffee, Josie considered his relationships with women. He'd dated, sure, but when she'd asked about any serious entanglements, he'd shrugged and shaken his head, as if getting serious wasn't important. Yet, he'd been with some pretty nice girls. It was almost as if he was scared of something.

He wasn't scared of getting close to Simone, that's for sure. The society princess was the woman of his dreams and he'd do anything to make her his wife.

Everyone needed a goal, and maybe it was time Josie found one of her own. Freelancing from home was great, but other than bowling and bingo, her life was pretty boring. Nothing like Simone the Socialite's.

Then again, Josie had followed Danny into all kinds of excitement. She'd tagged along when he'd bungee-jumped off a suspension bridge, and she'd taken pictures from the ground when he'd piloted his own hot-air balloon. They'd traveled overseas to France, Spain and England. There was always so much to do.

Unlike today, tomorrow or next week. These days she took her time and found comfort in everyday, mundane activities: her morning walk, throwing pennies in the fountain at the park, chasing Brutus, the chihuahua from down the block, out of her garden. Truth was, she'd had her fill of excitement…and loss.

"Shake it off, girl."

She studied her handwritten notes of basic themes and added to them, clicking away at the keyboard.

"Today we'll do Generous and Smart. Can you teach someone to be smart?" She shrugged. "Wednesday, Funny and Macho," she typed. "Thursday, Hear What

We Mean Not What We Say, and Thoughtful. Friday, we'll do Flowers for No Reason and Picking up After Yourself." She paused, remembering the state of Brett's apartment when he first made his love-lesson proposition. Old newspapers littered the entryway, a rolled-up undershirt lay balled on the counter, a half-eaten bag of chips littered the coffee table. "Better make that a day and a half."

They'd finish on Saturday with Hold Her All Night Long Without It Leading to Sex. The final exam and ultimate lesson men never seemed to get, even Danny.

They'd have sex anywhere and anytime if need be. He just couldn't wait, blaming it on his overactive libido. Sometimes she'd wished he'd spent more time touching her, gentling her. But then he had a lot on his plate, what with keeping the family business in order and pursuing his extracurricular activities.

She often craved more touching and lying quietly together, with no pressure of what would happen next, but she never admitted it. She figured the problem was hers, not Danny's. After all, he was the experienced one.

Last night, the feel of Brett's strong arms had warmed her heart. It came so naturally to him, holding her, making her feel safe.

Friendship must be the key. If Danny and Josie had been friends first they surely would have shared the same kind of intimacy.

Brett. Right. Her friend who needed her to get her head out of the clouds, for Pete's sake.

She finished typing the list of lessons and hit Print. It was only one o'clock. She had a few more hours until he got home from work. Time to get cracking on Nadine's stuff. She pulled out a six-inch-long, thin leather whip from the box and ran it between her fingers.

"What the heck?"

Just then someone knocked at the door. Funny, she hadn't buzzed anyone into the building. The front lock must be broken again, either that or Katy left it open so her daughters could run in and out without having to buzz.

She ambled through the living room, running the thin piece of leather across her palm. How was she going to write copy for this little item? *Guaranteed to keep your lover in line... With a snap of your wrist you can whip your lover into shape.*

"Police, open up!" Brett called from the other side of the door.

She unlocked the two dead bolts and pulled it open. "What are you doing here?"

"I'm a fast learner. I took the afternoon off like you ordered." He glanced at her hand. "A little harsh on the discipline, don't you think?"

"I'm working."

"I'll bet," he said with a smile. "Get your jacket."

"Why?"

"We're doing today's lesson outside. It's gorgeous. You're inside too much."

"But—"

"No buts," he said. "You're not making me waste this afternoon." He grabbed her denim jacket from the wooden rack by the door.

"Wait a minute," she said. "I was in the middle of something."

"Bring it with you." He eyed the whip and quirked a brow. "I'll help you practice."

"Very funny."

"Come on. Food's gonna spoil."

Brett watched Jo race around her already meticulous apartment, stacking mail, putting dishes in the washer, wiping down the kitchen counter.

"Keys, keys." He snapped his fingers.

"I'm getting to it." She straightened the mug rack so the one with purple hearts faced out.

"You're neurotic, you know that?" he said.

"There's nothing wrong with being organized. A woman likes an organized man, by the way."

Brett had a feeling his lack of organizational skills was the least of his worries.

She snatched her keys from the white bowl on the kitchen counter. "Got 'em. See, I know where everything is."

"Amazing."

She stood in the center of the room and looked right, then left. "Keys, jacket, answering machine, chicken defrosting for dinner—"

"Enough! Let's go."

"Where?"

"It's a surprise."

"Great, I'll get the list." She ran into her office and came out with a few sheets of white paper in hand. "Ready."

"It's a miracle," he said to the ceiling. He held her jacket so she could slip into it and caught a whiff of sweetness again, not raspberries this time, more like vanilla. Damn, made him hungry.

"You always smell good," he blurted out.

She pulled on her jacket and looked over her shoulder. "Thanks." Pink crept up her neck.

"Now I've embarrassed you. See? I'm always saying the wrong things."

"It was nice. I'm just not used to men complimenting me." She pulled the door closed and rattled the knob a few times for good measure.

He placed his hand around her wrist. "Stop, already. It's fine."

She froze, her back to him. He couldn't release her wrist but hadn't a clue why. To comfort her, maybe? He sensed her insecurity, her fear of her apartment being broken into. Had she been the victim of violent crime? Brett realized how little he knew about Jo, and it bothered him.

"I'm sorry if I made you uncomfortable, about the smelling thing," he said, feeling uneasy. But why? This was just Jo, his buddy.

"It's okay." She glanced into his eyes and smiled. That playful smile snapped him back to earth.

"Let's go." He released her wrist.

She nodded and they headed down the stairs to his truck.

"You going to tell me where we're going?" she said.

"You need to know that bad?"

"I guess not."

But he knew she did. Jo liked to feel in control at all times. He sensed it made her feel safe.

"We're going to the beach," he said.

"Haven't been there in a while."

They approached the truck and he reached for the door, but she beat him to it, climbing inside and closing it behind her. He hesitated, then walked around to his side of the truck. Damn, it irked him that she wouldn't even let him open the car door for her.

"Hey," he said, getting in and starting the engine. "Wasn't I supposed to open your door?"

She glanced at him. "Good point. Sorry, I'm not used to men doing things for me."

"You're not used to a lot of stuff," he said, turning onto Lake Street. "What, was this ex-husband some kind of deadbeat or what?"

When she didn't answer he glanced at her. She'd gone pale.

"Hell, I did it again, didn't I? I said something stupid." He hated that he could hurt her without even knowing it. She was sweet and honest, yet definitely guarded. Maybe with good reason if he kept doing stuff like this.

She touched the sleeve of his sweatshirt. "Don't worry about it. I'm tough, remember?"

He nodded, liking that she'd touched him. It meant she wasn't angry, that he hadn't hurt her as badly as he thought.

Jerk. He should avoid things he didn't understand, like her past and her husband. Her husband whom she was no longer with. That split must have been painful as hell. Look at how much pain his parents endured, yet they never split up. Pain was not something he wished upon Josie, ever.

"Listen, I brought a picnic lunch," he said. "I thought maybe you could pretend to be Simone." He read the pained look on her face. "Stupid idea. Scrap it. You're right, I'll just be myself and say a few prayers and let the chips fall where they may."

"It's okay. You took the day off for this. I'm impressed that you went to all this trouble." She eyed the picnic basket in the back seat. "Can't wait to see what you've got in there."

"Don't get too excited. I shopped for Simone, re-member?"

"You don't think I can appreciate the finer things in life?" She squared off at him and cocked her chin up a notch.

She was teasing, right? Or had he offended her again?

"I didn't mean that," he said. "I just meant, well, people have different tastes, in food, drinks and en-tertainment." He sounded like an idiot. Why was he self-conscious around Jo? She accepted him no matter what. That's the kind of relationship they had.

"You didn't pack any bologna sandwiches for me?" she said.

"Why are you busting my chops?" he said.

"Because they bust so easily." She smiled. "Okay, so I'm Simone." She stuck out her lower lip and raised an eyebrow. "What do you have planned for me today, hero-cop?" she imitated.

He couldn't help but smile. Jo was really getting into this. "How did you know about that nickname?" he said.

"I read a card she sent you."

"You shouldn't read other people's mail."

"What are you going to do, arrest me?" She winked. "What's on the agenda for today?"

"I thought I'd surprise you with a picnic by the lake. I've got a blanket so you won't get sand in your clothes."

"But she'll have to walk to the blanket," Josie said.

"Nah, I'll carry her."

"Nice."

"I'll spread everything out for her, feed her with my fingers—"

"You scrubbed them, right?" She grabbed his free hand and inspected his nails.

Warmth crept up his arm. "Knock it off." He pulled his hand back and clamped it on the steering wheel.

"So, you'll feed her caviar on expensive crackers, then what?" She jotted notes on the list of love lessons.

"You think she likes caviar?" he said.

"I don't know, she's your would-be fiancée."

"Hmm. Make a note of that caviar thing. Okay, after lunch we'll take a long, romantic walk along the shore, holding hands, talking, I guess."

"You guess?"

"I hate that mushy stuff," he said.

She laughed, that light, sweet chuckle of hers, then said, "If you don't talk mushy stuff, what do you normally talk about?"

"Me becoming a successful businessman. Her latest promotional event."

"How romantic."

"You're doing it again," he said.

"What?"

"Busting my chops."

"Right. Sorry."

But in truth, Josie couldn't help herself. For a remarkably handsome man the guy was completely clueless. She thought teasing him might be a more effective way of making her point: couples needed to talk about things other than business and social engagements. They should share their darkest fears, their most outrageous dreams.

Biting her lower lip, she glanced out the window. Not once had she told Danny about the modern-day fairy tales she wrote, stories based on hope and faith in mankind.

She hadn't told Danny because the whole thing sounded so corny and juvenile. Besides, her life revolved around being Mrs. Daniel Matthews, attending business dinners and fund-raisers.

It took a lot of energy to fit in where she knew, on some basic level, she never would. She'd smile, make small talk and ponder her latest fairy tale. Her smile was forced, her small talk practiced. But the emptiness in her heart was very real.

Brett turned into Gilson Park and drove slowly down the long, winding road. He found a parking spot overlooking Lake Michigan.

"I'd forgotten how beautiful it is here," Josie said.

"Romantic, don't you think?" He looked at her for approval.

"Yeah, romantic." Her gaze locked on his amazing aquamarine eyes. Some days she could see clear into his kind heart through those eyes. On other days the pain she read there scared the breath out of her.

"Should I kiss her?" He rested his hand on the back of her seat, so close he nearly touched the back of her neck. Her skin pricked with anticipation.

"Jo?"

"Huh?" Her heart thumped against her chest.

"Before we get out of the car? Should I kiss her?"

No! Yes! He's talking about Simone, silly. But I'm sitting right here. Is he going to kiss me if I say yes?

She panicked and flung open the door. "I'll have to think on that one," she called over her shoulder.

She took a deep breath and gazed across the lake

to the harbor. This whole thing was insane. She shouldn't be so darned nervous. He was imagining Simone in his car, eating his food, kissing his lips. Jo just happened to be the warm body that accompanied him as the understudy.

"You gonna make me carry all this?" he said, balancing a picnic basket, blanket and bottle of wine in his arms.

"Hang on, I'm coming." She walked around the car and took the wine and blanket.

"Thanks," he said, adjusting the basket and locking the car.

"Where to, chief?" She eyed the beach.

"There's a spot by the trees. I figured a little shade wouldn't hurt."

Nor would it melt Simone's makeup.

Behave, Josie.

She followed Brett to his special place, a place he'd obviously scouted out in advance for this occasion. They walked through a small mound of grass-covered sand and down to an isolated dip in the beach. He put down the basket, grabbed the blanket from her hands and spread it out.

"Well? What do you think?" he said.

"Very nice." She kicked off her tennis shoes and sat down.

With his pocket knife, he cut the seal from the wine bottle. "Just nice?"

"Nice is a good thing." She shaded her eyes from the sun with her hand. "What kind of wine?"

"Expensive," he said, as if that should be good enough.

"Does she like white wine?"

"I think so. Grab the glasses, will ya?"

She dug into the picnic basket and pulled out two crystal wineglasses. "Wow, where'd you get these?"

He took one from her and poured. "I'm not a complete loser. I do have nice things."

She didn't miss the offended tone of his voice. She took the glass and sipped. The dry wine tasted bitter on her tongue.

"Sure you don't want to sit down?" she said. "That chip on your shoulder must be getting pretty darn heavy."

He waved the bottle over her head, threatening to pour it on her hair.

"Might not be such a bad idea," she said. "I've tried everything else on this mop. Maybe wine would get it under control."

"It's not so bad," he said, then poured himself a glass and sat on the blanket. "Cheers."

They clinked glasses. He sipped his wine and shrugged. "Let's eat."

"Work first," she said. "Today's lesson is Generous and Smart."

"I buy her presents all the time."

"Being generous is not about giving presents. It's about being generous with your feelings. Letting her know you care about her. Ask questions about her life and be really interested in the answers."

"Like, 'How's work?'"

"That's a start." With pen in hand, she got ready to write.

Brett took another sip of wine, pursed his lips in distaste and swallowed. She suppressed a smile. He wasn't fooling anybody, least of all her.

God bless him for trying to fit into the life of someone he loved. She knew the feeling. She'd dressed the part, made the "right" friends and hosted dinner parties for prominent movers and shakers in the community. She'd tried so hard to fit into Danny's world.

"What else can you ask Simone?" she prompted.

"I guess I'd ask about her family, her parents and sisters, then about work," he said.

"What does she do?"

"Promotions for her dad's company. She also does some writing on the side. Speaking of which, how are your stories coming?"

He'd found out about her inspirational fairy tales the day her computer crashed and she'd thought she'd lost them all. Luckily Brett had talked her down from a full-blown anxiety attack, then found her a computer geek, someone's son from work, to save the day.

"They're coming along," she lied.

He narrowed his eyes at her.

"Okay, I've put them aside for a while," she confessed.

"Why?"

"The whole thing is…I don't know. Who wants to read modern-day fairy tales?"

"Maybe…I do?"

He smiled, that natural, warm smile, and she wanted to hug him. Sometimes, looking into his eyes, she thought anything was possible.

"You're my friend," she said. "You have to say that. Change of subject. What's for lunch? Anything good?"

"It'd better be good. It cost me enough." He opened the basket and pulled out a white container. "We'll start with—" he opened the lid "—oysters."

Being allergic to shellfish, her throat automatically started to swell. "Ah, Brett—"

"Then, marinated artichoke hearts, cracked crab legs, pickled herring and chocolate for dessert," he said.

She stared at the containers, feeling nauseous. Well, at least he'd brought chocolate.

"Here, darling," he said in a formal tone. "I'll start by feeding you an oyster." He pinched one of those little suckers between his fingers and it squirted out of his hand across the blanket. "Damn."

She smiled.

"Don't you laugh at me, woman."

"I'm shocked. You talk to Simone like that?"

"No," he said. "That's how I talk to you."

Her heart sank. She wondered how he talked to Simone.

"Let's give it another try." He stuck his hand in the oyster tub, trying to squeeze one between his fingers. "Oh, forget it. Make a note to substitute something else for oysters. Ready for artichoke hearts?"

"Actually…" She didn't have the heart to tell him she'd gagged on artichokes in the third grade and hadn't stomached one since.

"You don't like them?"

"I'll bet Simone loves them."

"She does," he said with such assurance, such pride, as if eating artichoke hearts was the ultimate proof that a woman was perfect.

"Okay, the main course," he said. "Cracked crab legs."

"Uh, Brett?"

He pulled out the container and peeked under the

lid. "Nothing moving in there. Okay, it's safe. Why do you think they call it cracked?"

He pulled out a crab leg and held it up for inspection. Shrugging, he aimed it in her direction.

"I can't," she said.

"You don't like crab, either?" he said, offended.

"I'm allergic to shellfish."

He dropped the crab leg into the container. "I'm striking out on all counts."

"Not with Simone. I'm sure she eats crab legs every day." Did that sound stupid or what? What did she expect? She'd been thoroughly rattled by the thought of Brett's fingers touching her lips.

"I know you like chocolate," he said. "At least that's one thing you and Simone have in common. Godiva okay?" He held up a piece of dark chocolate and aimed for her lips.

She started to protest, out of embarrassment more than anything, but he looked so determined to please, as if he'd be crushed if she rejected him. Or rather, if Simone rejected him.

Simone, right. Josie would act the part, which would effectively distance herself from the situation, plus it would give Brett some valuable practice. He placed the chocolate into her mouth and she moaned with pleasure. She closed her eyes and focused on the sweet flavor, letting it dissolve on her tongue, her lips still wrapped around Brett's forefinger. This is how Simone would do it. She'd suckle and lick until Brett was harder than granite.

Heavens, his finger tasted better than the gourmet chocolate. She moaned a little more for good measure and licked at his finger with the tip of her tongue.

"Josie!" He ripped his finger from her mouth.

She opened her eyes and swallowed the chocolate. "What?"

"What are you doing?" he accused, his eyes wide, his Adam's apple bobbing.

She liked the thought she had that kind of effect on him. "I'm eating chocolate."

"Like that?"

"Like what?" she challenged.

"Like…like…" he stuttered.

She burst out laughing. "I'm just messing with you. I was acting like Simone."

He shook his head and started shoving containers back into the basket. "This picnic was supposed to be a practice mission. It looks like I've already lost the war."

"Lighten up," she said. "What else have you got planned?"

"Never mind."

"Come on, don't be a spoilsport." She snatched another piece of chocolate.

"You're going to laugh," he said.

"Maybe not."

He shoved the basket to the corner of the blanket. "I was going to read poetry to her."

She studied his stubbled jawline, leading to full, remarkable lips.

"That's very romantic," she said.

"You sound shocked."

"That chip on your shoulder is growing by the minute."

He turned to look into her eyes. "It's really that obvious, huh?"

"Sometimes. When your guard is down." *When*

*you're with me like this, soaking up the sun, talking
about anything that comes to mind.*

"I thought I've kept it well hidden."

"You do, but I've picked up a few things in conversation. I figured you didn't grow up in Simone's
neighborhood."

"Maybe you should be the detective," he said,
sounding frustrated.

"Maybe we should take a break." She spotted a
playground over his shoulder a few hundred feet
away. She grabbed his hand. "Come on."

"But the lessons," he protested.

"We'll get to it." A part of her wanted to avoid
the love tutoring altogether.

She pulled him to his feet, then let go of his hand
and raced to the park. He came up behind her and
pinched her sides. She giggled and squeaked, then
hopped on the closest swing. It had been years since
she'd kicked her legs high on a swing, laughing with
the wind as it whipped through her hair. She didn't
dare act childish like this around Danny.

Brett gave her a push.

"I can do it myself," she said.

"I know you can." He pushed her again. "I'm just
trying to be nice. It's okay to let people be nice to
you, Jo."

"I guess."

"Jo?"

"Yeah?"

"Nothing."

"Jo?"

"Yeah?"

"Do you think the fact that I didn't grow up in a

wealthy family will work against me? Do you think that's why Simone is holding back?''

Josie swung higher, loving the free feeling, but not as much as the feel of his hands against her backside. Warm, solid hands. She'd miss those hands.

She took a deep breath. ''If you love someone, you love what's inside, not how much money they have or where they're from,'' she said. ''You should know that.''

''No, I don't. I've never loved anyone…before now.''

She swallowed hard, glad that she wasn't looking into his eyes for fear she'd read that gut-wrenching pain again. ''But you've been loved, by your parents, brothers and sisters?''

''Just one sister,'' he said. ''Yeah, I guess she loves me. But I was such a pain growing up, she'd probably never admit it.''

''Teased her a lot, huh?''

''Disciplined her a lot.''

''That's the parents' job.''

''Not my parents. They were…'' Brett hesitated, trying to decide if he should use the company line or tell the truth. ''Dad had a gambling problem and Mom was an alcoholic. They weren't around much, physically or emotionally, and when they were it wasn't pretty.''

There, he'd said it. He'd actually verbalized his feelings about his parents. He felt clean, yet raw. It felt damned good. Hell, he'd never told anyone what he'd just confessed to Josie. Not even his partner, and especially not Simone.

He waited for her reaction. A good minute passed.

All the old insecurities and shame flooded his chest. Damn, he shouldn't have—

"Bummer," she said, slowing down by dragging her bare feet on the sand.

She came to a stop and he offered his hand to help her off the swing. Taking his hand, she smiled, but it didn't reach those amazing amber eyes.

"Sometimes life isn't fair," she said.

He had a feeling she wasn't just talking about Brett's childhood. He wanted to ask about her life, her family. He wanted to know about her husband, mostly what the jerk did to cause the wariness in her eyes.

"I'm sorry." She wrapped her arms around his waist and hugged him.

Was it to comfort him or herself? The comment about his parents must have hit a nerve. Regret tore through him. He didn't mean to upset her. He'd just wanted to relieve some of the pressure building in his chest from years of anger and resentment that had, as Josie said, turned into one helluva chip on his shoulder. A chip that only she could see.

"I didn't mean to upset you," he said, stroking her soft blond waves.

She looked into his eyes. Sometimes she looked so young and vulnerable that he wanted to scoop her up and lock her in his apartment to protect her from the world. That would go over like pineapple on her pizza.

"You didn't upset me," she said. "I'm trying to comfort you. How am I doing?"

He laughed. "Hey, I thought you were the teacher."

"Not a very good one, I'm afraid." She held on to

him, her arms squeezing his waist, her breasts pressed against his chest.

He'd never noticed her breasts before, nor the light sheen of rose on her lips. Had she put on lipstick this morning or was that part of her natural beauty?

"Brett?" Her smile faded.

"Yeah?" His heart raced. Something was happening here. Something—

"I've thought about it," she said.

"What's that?" *Breathe, dammit.*

"You should kiss Simone whenever it feels right."

"Okay." He leaned forward and pressed his lips to hers. God, they were soft and tasted better than vanilla. The sweetness of chocolate lingered from the candy. And she fit perfectly against him, even being vertically challenged.

Her moan vibrated against his lips. He thought he was going insane. Kissing, tasting, holding…Jo?

As if she read his thoughts, she broke the kiss and jerked her hands from his waist. "Let's go get a hot dog."

She turned and started toward the blanket.

A hot dog? After what just happened? Wasn't she affected in the least by the kiss? Nah, it was all part of the lessons.

Jo put it in perspective for him. He and Jo were about hot dogs and playgrounds, not romantic picnics with expensive wine, or deep, wet kisses that turned his insides into mush and other parts into rock.

A good thing one of them still had some sense. This whole love thing was scrambling his brain.

Chapter Six

Brett eyed the menu board at Peeps Hot Dogs. "Well? What do you want?"

Now, that was a loaded question if Josie had ever heard one.

"A little of everything," she joked, trying to keep things light. Truth was, she hadn't recovered from his kiss. And that scared the hell out of her.

He pulled out a twenty and handed it to the cashier. "Three dogs with everything," he looked at Josie. "Fries?"

She shook her head.

"One large order of fries and two orange sodas," he ordered from the girl at the register.

"I'll get a table," Josie said.

She welcomed the opportunity to put some distance between them, even for only a few minutes. She found a booth in the corner and slid onto the hard plastic.

Mercy, that had been close. Way too close. What

was she thinking, giving him permission to kiss her like that?

Get real. He wasn't kissing you. He was kissing Simone.

When would she accept the fact that the time they spent together had nothing to do with her and everything to do with Brett snagging the woman he really wanted?

It was Josie's hormones, that's all. Raging, out of control. Dangerous, unwelcome hormones.

And one remarkable kiss.

"Here we go." He slid into the booth and placed her hot dog basket in front of her. "Sorry about lunch."

"What? Were they out of onions?" She analyzed her hot dog.

"I meant lunch number one."

"Oh." Grabbing some napkins, she tried to wipe lunch number one from her mind, especially that kiss. She absently placed a few napkins on his tray.

"Now you think I'm a slob?" he said.

She froze and looked at the inch-thick stack of napkins on his tray. Heavens, she couldn't think straight.

"It's always good to be prepared," she said with a smile.

"How many lessons have I failed so far?" He bit into his hot dog and relish plopped to the paper liner.

She pulled out the list and pretended to count, when in fact she struggled to forget the feel of his warm, firm lips on hers. She couldn't remember the last time she'd been kissed like that. It had been light years.

"That many, huh?" he said.

She glanced up. Had he read her mind? "What?"

"Lessons I've failed."

She snapped her gaze back to the list. "No, not really. You were generous today, planning the picnic, packing everything."

"Yeah, the wrong stuff." He shook his head and sucked pop through his straw.

"Not for Simone, it wasn't. This isn't about pleasing me, Brett."

And that rankled more than anything. For once in her life she wanted to be the center of a man's attention, to have him think about her and want to please her.

In retrospect, she'd been so enamored with Danny, almost infatuated, that she'd done all the pleasing. He rarely asked about her volunteer work at the center for the mentally handicapped, or her time spent planning a celebrity auction. He never asked what she was writing in her notebook late at night. Instead he'd tease her about having a boyfriend. He simply didn't take her needs seriously.

"Where are we at?" Brett said.

Right, on the list of lessons. "You're on the right track with Generous. Smart, well, that's another story," she teased.

"I'm more than halfway to getting my bachelor's degree. But I just haven't had time what with the new business and all."

"Don't worry about it. You're fine."

And he was. Smart, generous, caring, and then some. He was quite a catch.

She could even imagine herself falling for a man like Brett. A shudder ran across her shoulders. If falling in love meant losing herself again, she'd walk right past that hole, thank you very much.

"You in a draft?" he said. "You shivered."

"Too much ice in the soda," she lied. "Let's see, Funny and Macho, Thoughtful, Flowers for No Reason, ah, here, this one's going to take time—Picking Up After Yourself."

"I'm cooked."

"No, you're lazy."

"I'm busy."

"Aren't we all," she said, sarcasm lacing her voice. "Take a page out of my book."

"Wish I could, but you haven't finished it yet," he shot back.

"Leave me alone." She balled a napkin and tossed it at him. "Listen up. Being neat and organized is easy. If you take something out, put it back. Do it right away, don't wait until you can't walk through your kitchen without crunching spilled cereal beneath your shoes. Stay in the moment and stop thinking about what you have to do next."

His eyes glazed over.

"Brett, are you listening to me?"

"Yeah, kid, I'm listening." He placed his hand on the one she'd been writing with. Her breath caught.

"Keep talking," he said.

Talking, right. Sure. The heat from his hand raced up her arm. She couldn't even think, much less talk. She studied his eyes, which were intent on something over her shoulder. The jerk wasn't even paying attention to her.

"What, did Simone walk in or something?" She started to look over her shoulder.

"Don't turn around," he said. "Just keep talking."

"What's going on?"

"Nothing, yet."

It hit her like a bolt of lightning. He'd shifted into

cop mode. He watched a scene unfold at the counter, waiting for the right moment to intervene.

She slipped her hand from his and crossed her arms over her chest. She couldn't blame him for doing his job, but she could blame herself for drifting over the line, for starting to feel more than just friendship for him. It was too dangerous on too many levels.

"Everything okay?" she said.

"Probably. Just hang on."

Having lost her appetite, she studied his square jaw and slight squint to his eye. Nothing could divert his attention at this point. Probably not even Simone.

"Keep talking," he said.

"Don't start projects you can't finish. Have a designated place for everything and you won't lose things."

Like her heart. No, not her heart. Her common sense, more like it. After all, this man embraced danger, lived for it. She'd made herself a promise never to hurt like that again, never to fall in love and risk the pain that followed. If she acknowledged anything more than friendship for Brett she'd be stepping way over that line. She'd be walking into hell with her eyes wide open.

"Go on, get out of here," a male voice said. The manager, no doubt.

Brett's gaze followed someone out the door and across the parking lot. He blew out a deep breath and reached for his hot dog.

"False alarm." He took a bite and chewed heartily, as if he hadn't a care in the world.

Her stomach twisted into a knot.

"What's wrong? They put too much relish on it?" He motioned to her hot dog.

"No. I'm done. I'm ready to go whenever you are."

"Oh—" he hesitated "—okay. What about the rest of the lessons?"

"Here." She slid the sheet across the table. "Study it, memorize it. We'll review later."

"As in tonight, later?"

"Later this week."

"Tomorrow after work? How about dinner?"

"Can't tomorrow." She needed a night off, a whole twenty-four hours away from him so she could clear her thoughts and get her perspective back.

"What, you got a hot date or something?" he laughed.

She wasn't laughing. She couldn't laugh about the fact he thought it preposterous she'd attract a man, or that she hadn't had a man for way too long, or that deep down she liked the idea of Brett being her man. She especially wasn't laughing about that.

"I blew it again, didn't I? I hurt your feelings," he said, wiping his hands on a napkin.

If he reached for her hand she'd scream. She leaned back in the booth. "One of the most basic lessons a man needs to learn is that the world doesn't revolve around him. It's shocking, I know, but the truth is your snide remarks and jokes don't have any effect on me whatsoever."

He nodded, then pointed to her basket. "You gonna eat that?"

She pushed the half-eaten hot dog across the table. "Have at it."

Yep, *clueless* was the word.

Brett stuffed essentials in his backpack for his trip to the country with Josie. She talked a big game, but he knew her better than she knew herself. He'd upset her at Peeps the other day, even if she wouldn't admit it. Fact was, they hadn't spoken in nearly forty-eight hours, a record for them.

It couldn't be the kiss, could it? She'd invited him—directed him, more like it—to kiss her at the beach. He figured it was the Timing Is Essential lesson.

That was one lesson he probably should have skipped. Her lips tasted way too good, and her body, man, he could have held on to that body for a few more hours. Bad news. The whole kissing and holding thing. It didn't make sense. He'd never held Simone for more than a few minutes. What did he do differently with Josie that he could use on Simone?

He'd thought about this for the past two days, waiting for Josie to call with more instructions. But when he hadn't heard from her and she even relinquished her prized parking spot, he knew something was up. He had definitely upset her.

Well, today he'd fix all that. He'd take her to the country for an afternoon of riding and relaxation. No love lessons, no instruction and definitely no kissing.

She needed some time out of that apartment of hers and J.B.'s farm was the perfect place. Good thing work could spare him for the afternoon, a second afternoon off in more than a year. Back at the station, Mulligan had looked him over, wondering if Brett might be sick. Yeah, sick in the head over a woman.

He took the apartment steps two at a time, his heart pounding. He'd left Josie a message that he'd stop by around two for some emergency help.

He seemed to be needing her help a lot lately. He

hoped she'd open the door. It would be embarrassing as hell to have to break it down.

He stood outside her door and knocked three times. He waited for what seemed like hours.

Two dead bolts clicked and the door opened. "Hey," she said.

She looked smaller than usual, dwarfed in an oversize White Sox sweatshirt and baggy jeans. She wore some kind of ballet slippers on her tiny feet.

"Hi." He couldn't remember why he'd come.

"Everything okay?" she said.

"You got any boots?" Boy, did that sound stupid.

"Huh?"

"Never mind. Put on your sneakers, we're going out."

"I'm in the middle of something."

"Whips again?"

She smiled. His heart leapt.

"No whips," she said.

"Come on, Jo, please?" he said, only this time the begging didn't feel bad. "No lessons. Just fun. Promise."

"Okay, give me a minute."

She opened the door and he stepped inside. Her place was unusually messy, scattered newspapers stretched across her kitchen counter, and her blue-and-orange Bears afghan lay in a heap on the floor.

"Long night?" he said.

"Working." She came out of the bedroom wearing a tie-dyed T-shirt with a peace sign on the front and fire-engine-red tennis shoes.

"I picked up this magazine at the train station yesterday." He handed her the *Writer's Way Magazine*. "It has something about literary agents. I thought you'd need it for when you're ready to sell your fairy tales.''

"That was nice, thanks.'' She studied the cover for a second, then placed it on her coffee table.

"So, why the surprise field trip?'' she asked, grabbing her denim jacket from the rack.

"It's a thank-you for helping me.'' They stepped into the hall.

"I don't know how much help I've been.'' She jingled her keys in her pocket, shut the door and started down the stairs to the parking lot. No doorknob-jiggling this time.

"You've been a big help," he said, following her to the truck. He opened the door for her and she didn't protest.

He went around, got in the driver's side and started the engine. "I have complete confidence by this time next week I'll be putting an engagement ring on Simone's finger.''

"Positive thinking, I like that," she said. "But I'll have to get the darned thing off my finger first.''

He pulled away from the curb and wondered what else she liked, how else he could thank her for helping him snag the woman of his dreams.

A psychedelic T-shirt? Or maybe another cap to cover that unruly hair of hers. Not unruly, really, more like playful. She didn't wear a baseball cap today. A red headband that matched her shoes pulled blond waves away from her face. The girl had a style all her own.

"Have you been studying your lessons?" she said.

"Pretty much.''

"Okay, think you've mastered Generous yet?''

He turned onto Route 14. "Do I have to answer?''

She chuckled. "No sweat. Generous is a tough one for men. It's not your fault. Men naturally think about themselves first."

"And women don't?" he said, not appreciating the criticism of his gender.

"Women think about everyone around them, how they're feeling, what their needs are."

"You make us sound like coldhearted jerks."

"On some primitive level you were made that way to protect your loved ones. It's okay. We balance each other out."

She adjusted her body to face him, the seat belt straining against her breasts. He swallowed hard. He had to stop noticing things like that. Must be the tighter-than-usual T-shirt.

"Focus for a minute," she said.

"Focus, right." He settled his gaze where it should be, on the road ahead of him.

"Generous is about the giving of your time, your heart and your secrets."

Panic coiled in his gut. That would never happen. He'd never expose his shame, especially not to his would-be wife. She'd reject him for sure if she knew about his horrible family and low-class upbringing.

"Brett?"

He glanced at Jo.

"Generous. How can you be more generous?" she said.

"I don't know. Let me think about it."

For the next thirty minutes he did just that, silently. She must have sensed his discomfort because she kept trying to involve him in conversation about other things—work, apartment gossip, the Bears four-and-zero record.

Finally, he turned up the radio to signal he didn't want to talk. Even to her.

What the hell was the matter with him? Fear, that's what. Fear of losing it all to his secrets and faults. Fear that everything his parents had said was true: that he was no better than his parents and was destined to a life of anger and self-hatred.

As a kid he'd sworn to break free of that mold, to be a success and respect himself, unlike his parents. He'd live like the Tenderlins, rich with money and rich with love.

Out of the corner of his eye he noticed Josie studying his profile while chewing on the tip of her pen.

She turned down the radio. "Enough with the silent treatment. What did I do?"

He shook his head. "Nothing. I'm being a jerk, sorry."

"Oh, say it again."

"I'm sorry."

"No, the part about you being a jerk."

He smiled. She had a way of always making him do that at the strangest times, like when he came home at seven in the morning after filing a report on two underage teens injured in a drunk-driving accident. She'd brought him out of his funk with a smile and cup of hot chocolate. It was a gift.

"I'm not good at sharing my feelings," he admitted.

"Congratulations!" She reached out and patted his shoulder.

"What?"

"You're a typical male. Nothing to be ashamed of there. I'd be worried if you spilled your guts to me on a regular basis."

"You would?" he said.

"Sure. You done brooding?"

"I wasn't brooding."

"Yeah, you were. Guys are good at that."

"Yeah, and women are perfect?"

"Women sulk. Guys brood. There's a difference."

He shook his head in frustration as he turned up the gravel road to his friend's farm.

"Where are we, anyway?" she said.

"The Lazy Oaf Farm. Thought we'd go horseback riding and enjoy the Indian summer. There's a picnic lunch in the back, an extra jacket, wool blanket. J.B.'s got a quiet spot cleared out by the river where you can relax, take in nature, that kind of thing."

He pulled up to the barn and they got out of the car. Her eyes lit up as she scanned the ten acres of surrounding wooded land.

They approached the outdoor arena and he put one foot on the bottom rail of the metal fence. "What do you think?"

"Cool," she whispered, crossing her arms over the top rail and resting her chin on the backs of her hands.

"I thought you'd like it out here, seeing as you lived on a farm once," he said.

She nodded but didn't answer. Her gaze followed Brett's friend, J.B., as he gave a riding lesson to a young woman.

"That's my friend, J.B. This is his place."

No response.

"We knew each other in grade school, then his dad bought this place and they moved away. J.B. and I are trying to track down some of the old gang. We were a wild bunch in junior high school," he rambled. "Anyway, J.B.'s a lucky guy. This place is fabulous."

"Yeah," she said, her voice a mere hush.

He leaned down to look into her eyes. "Jo?"

Her eyes misted over. A pit balled in his stomach. "What?" He rubbed her arm and wanted to pull her to his chest, but something stopped him. Would she be offended at the gesture? Angry that he was trying to comfort her?

"Well, Detective, you've passed the 'thoughtful' part of the lessons with flying colors." She flung her arms around his neck and squeezed.

Chapter Seven

They stood there for what felt like ten minutes. Her cheek pressed against his chest, her arms wrapped tight around his neck. He didn't know what caused the emotional outburst, but he didn't mind. Considering his height and her lack of, they were quite a comfortable match.

He held her close, his hands clasped at her lower back. She didn't seem like she was moving any time soon. Strange that he couldn't remember holding Simone for any length of time like this. Yet he must be doing it right or Jo would have corrected him. One more lesson in the list of many.

"You're very nice to have brought me here," she said, her voice muffled by his leather jacket.

Her arms tightened around his neck, as if offering a parting squeeze. He didn't want to let go.

"I wanted to do something special for you, something to say thanks for helping me," he said.

Something they would both remember. Once he

and Simone were married, there'd be no place in his life for Jo. Regret coiled in his gut. He pushed it aside.

"Hey, Callahan, you planning on riding?" J. B. Lechner said, riding up to them on a beautiful Appaloosa.

Jo broke the embrace and stepped back, wrapping her arms around her midsection as if chilled. Embarrassed, more like it.

"J.B., this is Josie Matthews," Brett said.

J.B. tipped his hat and smiled. "Nice to meet you, ma'am. I've heard a lot about you."

"No, I'm not his girlfriend."

"I know that, darlin'. And it's a good thing." He winked.

Oh, brother. What was with the guy? Must get lonely out here on the farm, Brett thought.

Jo rocked back on her heels and smiled at J.B. He leaned forward in his saddle and leered. Brett controlled the sudden urge to step in between them.

But why? They were both single. J.B. never married due to the grueling life of taking care of a farm and training horses. His lack of social skills was apparent in his behavior today.

"We're ready to ride," Brett interrupted.

"So you are," J.B. said.

Brett could have sworn the cowboy licked his lips.

"Have you got two horses ready?" Brett prodded.

J.B. ignored Brett and just smiled at Josie. Her gaze drifted to the ground, where she toed the dirt with her red tennis shoes.

Shy, gentle, alluring. Brett blinked twice. Where did that come from? He'd never noticed a single feminine quality about Jo before. Playful, maybe, fun-loving and even tough at times, but alluring?

"Horses?" he said to break whatever spell J.B. had fallen under.

"Heard ya the first time," J.B. said. "I'm thinkin' I'd better come along. The woods get a little tricky around Burton's Pass. You'll need a guide."

Like hell they did. The guy just wanted to make time with Jo. Well, forget that. He'd brought Jo out here to relax and enjoy the scenery, not fight off a lonely cowboy.

"I was out here two months ago," Brett said. "Can't imagine the woods have changed that much."

"Probably not, but it wouldn't hurt to have a chap-erone." He looked at Josie. "This man might be a cop, but I hear he's got a way with the ladies. I wouldn't trust him if I were you."

"Thanks, but we don't have that kind of relation-ship," she said.

"Why not?" J.B. said with another wink.

Brett balled his hand into a fist. He had the sudden urge to give the cowboy a black eye.

"How about those horses?" Brett said in as normal a tone as he could muster. His buddy was really get-ting on his nerves.

J.B. smiled one last time at Jo and trotted off, ever the expert horseman. Only when he was out of sight did Brett's blood pressure return to normal. What was that about? Protective instinct, that's all. He consid-ered Jo a good friend and didn't want her getting charmed by a cowboy. She seemed so gullible just now, soaking up J.B.'s sweet words. Brett had to step in and protect her.

Who was going to protect her when Brett was no longer around?

"He's nice," Josie said.

"Nice isn't exactly how I'd describe him today."

"How would you describe him?"

"Flirtatious. The jerk was coming on to you."

"He was just being polite." She ripped the headband from her hair and shook it out. The wind blew golden strands off her forehead. Closing her eyes, she tipped her head back, letting the wind brush across her face.

If J.B. saw this it would be a threesome ride for sure.

The thought of J.B. holding Josie, kissing her, shot fire through Brett's chest.

"Come on, we'll saddle our own horses." He started for the barn.

"Hey," she said, grabbing his jacket sleeve.

Her touch made him want to pull away even more. He didn't know why.

"I'm sorry if I made you uncomfortable before, with the hugging and stuff," she said. "It was just really nice, bringing me here."

"Yeah, just watch it or you'll be charmed right out of your saddle by J.B."

They ambled toward the stalls.

"You're imagining things," she said.

"Don't be naive, Josie. It's not like you."

"And don't be paranoid. We both know men don't look at me like that."

He slowed his step and she breezed past him.

"Like what?" he said.

"Like you look at Simone," she called back. "I'm just not the sexy type."

She disappeared into the barn. She was right. He didn't look at her like *that*. He'd never looked at her like that. But other men could recognize natural beauty when they saw it: her warm smile, sparkling eyes and playful personality. Other men would be crazy not to notice the golden-blond highlights in her hair and makeup-free, creamy complexion. The same men who were drawn to the down-to-earth look, a down-to-earth woman.

But not Brett. He knew what he needed to make his life complete. A classy woman—in his case, Simone Trifarra.

Yet he wasn't going to let Josie's innocent nature lead her into the arms of a randy cowboy. She was helping him snag the woman of his dreams; the least he could do was protect her from the wolves of the world. Just like a big brother would.

He grabbed his backpack full of lunch supplies from the truck. Heading for the barn, he secured the pack across his shoulders. Ham-and-cream-cheese roll-ups, garlic pickles and marshmallow-fluff chocolate candy. Three of Josie's favorites. He'd planned it just right. Except for the unexpected attention of J. B. Lechner.

Stepping into the barn, he froze at the sight of them and wondered if the wolf hadn't already claimed its prey. Josie sat on a bale of hay swinging her legs, fascinated by J.B. as he saddled a horse.

They looked perfect together. Horse people. Hanging out, sharing, bonding.

"If Dad had lived a few more years I probably would have talked him into selling the place. But I couldn't do it once he was gone." J.B. grunted as he cinched up the horse. "Not without his blessing."

"Why would you want to sell? It's great out here. The horses, the fresh air." A black-and-white mutt scampered up to her. "Even you." She slid off the bale and scratched the dog's ears.

J.B. stared at her, his fingers frozen on the leather strap. "It's lonely," he blurted out.

She glanced at J.B., compassion in her eyes.

"We ready to go?" Brett said, feeling like the fifth wheel. They looked at him with blank stares, as if neither understood the language he spoke.

"Riding? We're going riding, remember?" he said.

"Almost done," J.B. said, recovering.

Brett glanced at Josie. Loneliness dimmed her usually playful eyes. But why? She had friends, a great job working from home, an active dating life. He'd seen men come and go from her place, laughing, joking. If there was one thing Josie could do well it was make a person smile.

But right now she wasn't smiling and that bothered him. A lot.

"You take the stallion. Josie can take the Appaloosa," J.B. said, handing Brett the reins. "Lead him out. We'll follow."

Brett hesitated, once again feeling like the fifth wheel. Would J.B. and Josie share another sacred moment, a hidden emotion that only two lonely people understood?

Why hadn't Brett noticed the loneliness before? Was he dense?

Josie and J.B. came out of the barn. "Need help getting up?" J.B. offered Josie, who held the Appaloosa's reins in her hands.

"No," Brett said.

"Sure," she countered.

J.B. was the perfect gentleman, not touching Josie in any inappropriate ways as he hoisted her into the saddle. Brett had to give him credit. He wasn't sure how many men could behave with her round fanny so close to the touch. Then again, J.B. knew Brett carried an off-duty firearm in his boot.

Brett shoved his foot into the stirrup and pulled himself up.

"Her name's Star," J.B. instructed Josie. "She's a special one, gentle, just like you."

Gentle? Josie? She smiled and squeezed the reins. Something knotted in Brett's gut.

"Let's go," Brett said with a kick to the horse's ribs.

The animal grunted but didn't budge.

J.B. let out a howl of laughter. Josie coughed to mask a giggle.

"What?" Brett said.

"You're on Sergeant. He's a bullheaded animal, not that you can relate to that."

"Does the beast have a first gear?" Brett said.

"Oh, he's got more than that. I hope you don't find out just how much." J.B. smiled at Josie again.

What was that, ten times? Brett shoved back his irritation. He wanted to be out in the wilderness with Josie by his side.

"Star should lead and Sarge will follow," J.B. said. "Typical story of a love-struck animal."

Josie chuckled.

"Great, now I'm getting love lessons from a damn horse," Brett muttered.

"What's that?" J.B. said.

"Forget it. Ready?" Brett said to Josie.

She shot J.B. one last smile. Enough, already. With

the reins in her right hand and her left hand settled on the saddle horn, she guided Star onto the trail.

A few minutes into the ride the tension in Brett's shoulders uncoiled. Probably because he'd saved Josie from that ladies' man.

Brett had never thought of J.B. as a playboy before. Yet the immediate connection between Josie and J.B. was obvious.

How could that be? It's not like they'd had months or years to get acquainted. They didn't know each other's favorite foods or secret phobias. Josie and J.B. knew nothing about each other. Nada. Zip. Zero. Brett should stop worrying. Josie was safe.

She turned, her left hand on the horse's rump, her hair flying around her face. "It's beautiful out here."

"I'm glad you like it."

"Where are we going?"

"In about ten minutes we should hit a clearing overlooking a waterfall."

"Out here?" she said, amazement filling her voice.

"Yep."

"You're just full of surprises."

"Yep. Who knows, maybe I'll surprise you in the love department."

Her lips curled into a forced smile and she turned her back to him. His chest went cold. How could he know her so well, yet not have a clue as to what she was thinking right now?

That's it. Once they got to their destination, he'd press her for the truth, find out why she was acting so strangely. Heck, she nearly came apart in his arms back there. That wasn't simple gratitude. There was something more to the embrace. Something that set off alarms in his head and an edginess in his gut.

Studying her body as she naturally swayed with the gait of the horse, he decided he'd also discover what caused the loneliness in her eyes. They'd been friends for nearly two years and he'd never seen that look before. Then again, maybe he'd never paid close enough attention.

It seemed he was paying attention to a lot of things he didn't normally notice: how her round bottom filled out her worn jeans; how the sun picked up highlights in her hair; how her breasts rounded out the peace sign on her T-shirt just right.

He was a healthy man who'd been without a woman for way too long. Of course, he'd notice things about a warm-blooded woman, a woman he'd only thought of as the gal upstairs. The look in J.B.'s eye made Brett want to wrap her under his wing for protection.

But she was a big girl. She'd been married and divorced and had her share of boyfriends. It wasn't as if she needed Brett's help. Did she?

"I think I see it," she called over her shoulder. Star slowed to a stop and Josie hopped down, wrapping the reins around a sturdy tree branch.

"Hang on," he said, but she'd quickly disappeared into the brush.

He dismounted and secured the reins to a tree. Sarge snorted in disgust. "Yeah, and who made you Casanova King?"

Giving the horse an affectionate pat to his neck, Brett adjusted his supplies and headed after her.

A high-pitched squeal shot panic across his shoulders.

"Josie!" he called, racing into the brush where she'd disappeared. His gut balled into a knot at the thought of her being hurt, of not being able to protect her.

"Jo!" He raced through the wooded path, branches slapping his face.

He broke through the clearing overlooking the waterfall and scanned the immediate area.

Then he heard it. The sound of a woman laughing.

Five feet below, along the riverbank, he spotted Josie sitting in a puddle of mud. Her blond hair was streaked gray, her face dotted with dirt. Big clumps of mud decorated her denim jacket and jeans. But she was okay. He took a relieved breath. Then anger rose in his chest.

"You scared the hell out of me," he said.

"I am such a klutz," she said, laughing. "Join me?"

"Get back up here," he demanded, so he could see up close that she was okay.

She got to her feet and wavered. His gut tightened.

"You're hurt?" he said.

"I'm fine. The ground isn't very solid down here."

"Give me your hand." He knelt down and reached for her hand.

"You're really mad at me?" she said with sad, apologetic eyes.

"I'm not mad. Now, come on, give me your hand."

"What a role reversal. I'd usually freak about getting all full of muck and you'd be laughing."

"Your hand," he demanded.

She hesitated, and he wondered what the heck was the matter with her.

"You're not going to give me a lecture, are you?"

"Josie, just give me your hand."

She wrapped her fingers around his wrist and he did the same. The connection was unusually warm—hot, even. His body tightened in places it shouldn't. *Get a grip, Callahan.*

"You're a mess," he said, hoping an insult would derail his inappropriate reaction to her. He slowly pulled.

"Lesson number twenty-seven," she said. "Never tell a woman she's a mess when she's a mess. Always tell her she looks beautiful."

Actually, she didn't look that bad for having just gone two rounds with the muddy earth. No, she looked incredibly healthy, refreshed, even happy.

"You look—" he jerked her up next to him "—beautiful."

Even covered with mud she smelled good—sweet, yet spicy, like cinnamon? Her body felt small and so fragile against his. He held on.

"You really think so?" she said, her voice a mere hush.

He couldn't remember what they'd been talking about. His mind spun with images of gently removing her dirty clothes and wrapping her up in a soft flannel blanket. Of washing the mud from her blond waves and toweling them dry. Of brushing dirt from her cheek and kissing the red mark where she'd scratched it.

"Your cheek." He cupped her chin with his forefinger and thumb and tipped her face to get a better look.

"I must have scratched it going down."

"Does it hurt?" He brushed it gently with his thumb.

She blinked, slowly, gripping the lapels of his

leather as if he were a life preserver. She must be scared. Or seriously hurt and not admitting it.

In one swift motion, he picked her up.

"Hey!" she protested.

"Your clothes are soaked. We'll build a fire and warm you up."

"Don't carry me. You'll hurt yourself."

"I've carried heavier."

"Gee, thanks."

"You're welcome." He couldn't look at her, couldn't bear to see more evidence of injury.

"What the hell were you trying to do, anyway?" he said.

"See the water better."

"You could have drowned in the river." He stepped over a downed tree branch and headed for the makeshift campsite.

"Hey, let's make this your macho test. Man carries wounded woman five miles to safety. Check." She pretended to make a check mark with a pencil.

"This is funny to you?"

She poked him in the chest. "Lighten up."

Gritting his teeth, he made his way to the campsite J.B. had designed for his friends.

"You're a big crab today," she said. "I'm clumsy. I fell. I didn't hurt anything important."

He sat her on a bench carved from a tree trunk and she winced.

"That's it," he said. "I'm getting the horses."

"No!" She grabbed his sleeve. "Don't let my clumsiness ruin this day. It's beautiful out here."

He paced a few feet away and back again. "Tell me where you're hurt."

"I'm not hurt." She crossed her arms over her chest.

"I'm getting the horses."

"Okay, okay." She sighed. "I bruised my hip."

He narrowed his eyes.

"I might have twisted my ankle a little. It's embarrassing to admit this, okay?"

"Why?" He pulled the pack from his shoulders. "It's not like you're admitting you have a drinking problem or something."

He knelt down and started to unlace her shoes.

"What are you doing?"

"Gotta check for swelling."

"I'm okay, really."

He took off her shoe and sock. No swelling. That was good, but he'd keep an eye on it over the next hour.

"Take off your jacket," he said.

"Why?"

"It's wet. You'll wear mine."

She did as ordered, grumbling under her breath. "I hate this."

"What?" He cloaked her small frame in his extra-large leather jacket.

"I'm not big into needing people, in case you haven't noticed."

"Is that why it didn't work with your ex-husband?" He couldn't believe he'd said the words. "I'm sorry, that was out of line."

He turned away from her and started building the fire, having surely failed the sensitivity test. What the hell had gotten into him?

He shouldn't have asked. Her answer shouldn't be so important. But it was.

Josie watched Brett strategically set up the logs, stuff kindling beneath them and start the fire. Her heart went out to him. It must be frustrating to know so much about a good friend, yet know so little. Did he think she kept secrets because she didn't trust him?

She couldn't stand the thought. Of all the people in her life, she trusted Brett more than anyone.

"Is your shirt wet?" he asked, his back to her.

"No, it's fine."

"You look cold. Put this on." He unbuttoned his denim shirt.

"I'm okay, really."

He walked toward her, his solid chest muscles straining against the white undershirt. Hard muscles just right for a woman's touch. She glanced at the hot embers. "I don't want your shirt."

"And I don't want you catching a cold."

He slipped his jacket from her shoulders, handed her his shirt and waited for her to button up. The sleeves hung way below her hands; the shirttail practically touched her knees.

"I look like a kid playing dress-up in Dad's clothes."

"Here." He put the jacket back around her shoulders. "You look beautiful," he said, repeating her words of advice from a moment ago.

"You're a fast learner."

He crouched by the fire and gave it a poke with a branch. "Are your pants wet?"

"Enough, already. You may not be generous with your feelings, but you sure are generous with your clothes."

"Clothes are easy. Opening up, that's another story."

Didn't she know it. She'd accused him of not being generous with his feelings, yet she'd kept her own hidden pretty well. Maybe it was time to show him generosity by example. But could she risk it?

"He's dead," she blurted out. Talk about awkward.

Brett stood and turned to her, a kindling stick dangling from his fingers.

"Who?"

"My husband."

The stick dropped to the ground.

"It's okay. It was a long time ago. Five years, actually."

"How?"

"Freak accident, skydiving. Danny was into some crazy stuff to release the pressure of family responsibilities. He ran the family's real estate business, among other things."

"I thought you were divorced," he said.

"Not divorced," she said. "Danny was my one and only true love. I haven't seriously dated since the accident."

"But the men who come and go from your place—"

"Clients. They drop stuff off sometimes."

"Why didn't you tell me?"

"I didn't see the point. It doesn't affect our relationship."

Or did it? she wondered.

"I don't know what to say. I'm...sorry." He shoved his hands into his jeans pockets and glanced at the fire.

She jumped to her feet, ignoring the dull pain in her ankle. The jacket fell from her shoulders to the bench, but she didn't care about the chill. "Don't you dare start with the pity or I swear I'll quit the bowling team.''

''What are you talking about?''

''When Danny died I was empty inside, felt as if I didn't exist if I wasn't Mrs. Daniel Matthews. I'd depended on him for so many things, even my self-esteem. I put everything into our marriage, and after he died I had nothing. Then I had to deal with the resentment from his family and the pity from mine. 'Poor Josie lost her prince, now where will she go? What will she do? Poor Josie, come home and let your big brothers take care of you.' I couldn't stand it so I started a new life here in Arlington, depending on no one but myself. I had to get away from his judgmental family and my smothering one. I don't need pity from anyone. And I sure as hell don't want it from you.''

She grabbed the backpack and dug through it, for what, she didn't know. ''Got anything for lunch?''

He draped his jacket across her shoulders. ''You must be cold.''

''I don't feel a thing.''

''Jo?''

''What?'' She couldn't look at him, not after the emotional outburst. That wasn't like her. She guarded her feelings, shunned her pain.

He turned her to face him and pulled her against his chest.

''Don't.'' She pressed her hands to his chest and looked into his eyes.

''Why not?'' he said.

''I told you, I don't want your pity.''

''I think this is called compassion, Josie.''

Threading his fingers through her hair, he guided her cheek to the hard planes of his chest.

Closing her eyes, she inhaled the rich scent of man and struggled not to come undone in his arms. But all the repressed feelings, all the denial of the past five years welled up inside and threatened to burst her chest open.

He stroked her hair. "I wish you'd felt comfortable enough to tell me the truth about your husband."

Not comfortable enough? More like, too comfortable.

The truth struck her square in the face: she hadn't felt any kind of bond with a man since before or after Danny had come and gone from her life.

Until she'd met Brett.

She clung to his shirt, drowning in the realization that she'd not only lost the man she loved five years ago, but if she wasn't careful she'd fall in love with another man she was destined to lose. To his job, to another woman, what did it matter? She couldn't handle that kind of pain again.

"I'm sorry, I don't usually fall apart like this," she said, pushing away from him and forcing a smile.

"It's okay. You can fall apart on me anytime. That's what friends are for."

Chapter Eight

Friends.

The word shocked her back to earth. Secretly wanting more wouldn't change the fact she could never be with Brett. It also wouldn't change the fact he loved another woman.

"I wish I had a boatload of friends like you," she said.

"Sometimes all you need is one."

"Thanks." She gave him a friendly squeeze and stepped away, afraid if she stood too close, too long, she'd throw common sense aside and fall into his arms again.

"You sure you're okay?"

"I'm fine," she said.

"I brought your favorites." He smiled and held the backpack open for her.

She could tell he was trying to cheer her up.

She dug her hands inside and pulled out a bag of candy. "Marshmallow fluff!"

"Don't you think you should eat your entrée first?"

"Which is?" She settled herself on the bench.

"Ham-and-cheese roll-ups."

"Yum. But I'm in the mood for dessert. What did you bring for yourself?"

"Hey, there're four pounds of fluff in there. You don't plan on eating it all by yourself, do you?"

"I don't know, I'm pretty hungry," she said.

"That's one of the things I like about you. You're not neurotic about what you eat."

"In other words, I'm a pig."

"I didn't say that." He sat next to her and pulled a can of soda from the backpack. "It's just, once in a while I'd love to take Simone to Peeps for a hot dog with everything."

"She's not into fast food?" Josie bit into the chocolate chunk filled with marshmallow.

"When we go out she orders a salad made of dark green leaves and unidentifiable vegetables. Once in a while I wouldn't mind going out for a cheeseburger." He tossed a stick into the fledging fire.

"Now, Detective, you have to love her, faults and all. No one's perfect." She handed her the cola and she took a sip.

"Don't I know it," he said.

"Meaning what?"

"Obviously I'm not perfect or she'd be Mrs. Callahan by now."

"You really think she'll take your name?"

He stared her down. "Why? What's wrong with my name?"

"Nothing, it's just with a last name like Trifarra, well, she may not want to give up the prestige."

"Tough. If she's my woman, she'll change her name."

"My, aren't we sounding prehistoric," she teased, poking his arm.

"I can't help it. I just know how things should be."

"Like you know what kind of woman you should marry?"

"Exactly."

"Then we'd better get to work. You passed the macho test by breaking your back carrying me. Let's see, what's next…" She tapped her forefinger to her chin.

Brett smiled to himself. She was teasing. It amazed him that she could recover her sense of humor so quickly after talking about her late husband, her one and only.

A hollowness filled his gut. Losing her husband must have been devastating. She was one remarkable woman to bounce back from that.

But had she? She didn't date so she must still be recovering. Either that, or no man on earth would compare to her one and only love. His chest tightened at the thought. Would any woman love him like that? So completely that she couldn't even consider being with another man? Simone surely didn't. Not yet, anyway.

"Sentimental, compassionate, macho…" she recited.

"We're stuck on generous, I know," he said.

Her amber eyes widened and she touched his bare arm. The innocent contact burned a trail up to his heart.

"You're generous in many ways," she said. "You're okay."

He wished she was casting judgment on his soul, not his romance skills. He swallowed hard. Since when did her opinion matter so much?

"The way you held me before and listened to me. That was very generous," she said. "I know it had to make you uncomfortable."

It should have, she was right. Instead, it felt natural, if not a bit painful. The thought of her loving a man so much that she hadn't dated since his death tangled Brett's insides into a knot. Could it be envy that no woman had ever felt that way about him? Or was he developing stronger, inappropriate feelings for Jo?

"I shouldn't have unloaded like that," she said.

"You're a good friend. It's my job to listen to you." *Just a friend,* he reminded himself.

She smiled, but melancholy tinted her eyes. He should stop this now. It had to be painful for her to think about love when it had been stripped from her life.

Her one and only. His gut constricted.

"Josie, maybe we should—"

"Mind reading," she interrupted.

"What?"

"It's time you learned to read our minds."

"That's ridiculous." He grabbed a ham-and-cream-cheese roll-up.

"Not ridiculous. You just have to think like a woman."

"No, thank you. Pretty soon I'll be worrying about the size of my butt and the four strands of gray hair I discovered last month."

"You're turning gray?" she cried with joy. "Where?" She leaned forward to poke through his hair.

"Knock it off." He batted her hand away. "I don't want to think like a woman, obsessing about having said the wrong thing to the chairman of some charity board, or not wearing the right designer shoes to a swanky fund-raiser. Hell, it'll drive me nuts."

"Is that what Simone worries about?"

"Yeah." He shrugged. "Sometimes I feel like I'll never understand women."

"Oh, come on. You've dated."

"Recreational stuff."

"Ick." She shuddered.

"What, ick?"

"That sounds so callous."

"What, was I supposed to fall in love with every one?"

"Sorry, I guess I just can't relate, having been with one man."

"Your one and only," he whispered.

She glanced into the fire, her eyes distant. He guessed memories haunted her, or was it regret? He couldn't be sure.

"Do you want to talk about it?" he said.

"What?"

"Your husband."

She looked into his eyes and he wanted to hold her again. But he didn't want her to think pity motivated him.

"He was my Prince Charming," she started. "He gifted my life with excitement and opened my eyes to a new world. He went to college in my hometown. I waitressed at the twenty-four hour pancake house to work my way through school. It was...love at first sight, for me, anyway."

"And him?" Damn, he wished they'd change the subject.

"Same for him. We dated for a year until his graduation. His parents weren't happy. They had this idea of the perfect girl for Danny and it wasn't me."

How could anyone not immediately like Josie? "What was their problem?"

"Typical stuff. I'm not from money so they accused me of being a gold digger. I'm not sophisticated, as if you haven't noticed." She fingered her mud-encrusted hair. "I wasn't a showpiece wife."

"There's a lot more to it than that."

She chuckled.

"What?" he said.

She shook her head and took a deep breath. "Anyway, I did my best to fit in. I joined social clubs and did a lot of volunteer work. Even dressed the part. But in the end, you can't change what a person is—" she paused and placed an open palm to her chest "—here."

Right, his biggest fear.

"Then he died and everything fell apart," she said. "I had no life. His family acted as if it was my fault. They especially didn't like that he'd left me a decent sum of money in his will." She crossed her arms over her chest and stared into the fire. "Like I wanted the money."

"It must have been hard."

"Yeah, it was. I thought I was going to die right along with him. But it's been five years. The pain isn't so bad anymore. It lessens with time, I guess."

But the love would never lessen.

"Anyway, enough of this morbid talk. We're out

here to have fun. How about my most favorite lesson?''

''We're taking the day off, remember?'' He didn't know if he could stand talking about love anymore, being reminded how far he was from something so wonderful.

''You're going to like this one.'' She slapped her hands to her thighs. ''Hear What We Mean, Not What We Say.''

He'd done that just now, heard the meaning of her words: she'd loved once, completely, and hadn't dated since. That one love was enough. His chest ached.

''If Simone mentions her favorite flower, it means she wants a dozen,'' she said.

He wished she'd stop talking. He needed time and space to process things.

''If she comments on a review of the newest Broadway show, you'd better take her,'' she offered.

''No more shows,'' he said.

''Take a No Doz.''

''Forget it. They're boring.''

''Not all shows. You just have to find what you like.''

''I'm not that kind of guy.''

''What kind of guy?''

''A cultured guy.''

''You don't have to be cultured to like music. Look at me.''

He did, and couldn't help but burst out laughing.

''What?'' She crossed her arms over her chest, indignant.

''Sorry, but you don't look very cultured right now. Maybe it's the hair.'' He reached out and fingered a clump of blond, glued together with gray muck. "I've got a comb in my inside pocket of the jacket you're wearing."

He started to reach for it, but his hand came up short. It felt wrong for his hand to be so close to her breast. His fingers itched.

She pulled the comb from his jacket. "I hate these things."

"Combs?"

"My hair is a bit thick, in case you haven't noticed."

"And wild."

"Thanks for pointing that out." She smirked and stuck the comb in her hair.

"I didn't mean—"

"New lesson—if you can't compliment a woman's hair, keep your mouth shut."

He watched her dig the comb into the mass of blond and grit her teeth.

"Let me do it," he said.

"No, thank you."

"Why not? I'll comb your hair while you rattle off mind-reading skills." He snatched the comb and stood behind her.

"Don't you hurt me."

"Which really means, hurt me?" he teased. "Relax, I used to comb my baby sister's hair all the time."

Pressing the teeth of the comb into the blond waves, he eased the muck out of her hair, a few strands at a time.

"Am I hurting you?" he said.

"No. Keep going." Her head lolled to the side.

"Which means stop?"

"Yeah, stop being a jerk and comb my hair."

He did, for a good ten minutes. He was a master hair-comber from years of practice taking care of Lacy when his mom was too drunk to be bothered, and his dad was out gambling away what little family money they had.

"I'm gonna be rich!" his father would shout, racing out the front door. His mom would grab the bottle of booze and disappear into the bedroom. Brett noticed that his dad never said, "*We're* going to be rich."

Maybe that was Brett's problem. Maybe he was a selfish bastard like his dad and no one had the guts to tell him.

"Why did you stop?" Josie asked, jarring him from his thoughts.

He didn't realize he'd stopped combing her hair.

"Sorry. Got to thinking about stuff," he said.

"Simone?"

"Believe it or not, I'm not obsessed with the woman."

"Uh-huh."

He refocused on his task, freeing Josie's hair of hardened mud. The dirt completely gone, her hair was back to its normal wavy mass, highlighted with streaks of gold, like spun sunlight. He couldn't stop combing. The sounds coming from her throat didn't help. To give this kind of pleasure was a real kick. The texture of her hair surprised him as he ran the smooth strands between his fingers.

"If I say 'You can stop combing my hair,' what do I mean?" she asked.

"Keep combing?"

"Good boy. If I say 'I have no problem going to the bowling party by myself,' I mean…"

"You want me to go with you."

"Hmm. You're pretty smart," she said. "Don't let anyone tell you different."

"But there's still one major problem."

"What?"

"I can't tell her how I feel."

"A little practice…you'll get it…." Her voice trailed off.

Brett feared that in a minute his tutor would be fast asleep. It seemed to be a habit around him. He stopped combing and sat down next to her.

Her eyes fluttered open. "What?"

"I want to practice."

She sighed. "Okay, pretend I'm Simone again."

He took her hand and noticed it trembled. "You're cold."

"I'm fine. Stop stalling."

"I can't help it. I don't know what to say."

"Tell her how you feel about her, what you love about her."

He cleared his throat. "I think you're classy, intelligent and sexy. You're an impeccable dresser, you always know what to say in any social situation, you believe in my new business, you—"

"Stop!"

"What?" He let go of her hand.

"How do you feel about her as a person? You know, does she make you smile, accept you unconditionally? That kind of stuff."

"Mushy stuff," he grumbled.

"Face it, big guy, we might be tough on the outside, but we're mush on the inside."

"I can't do this," he said.

"Why not?"

"You'll laugh at me."

You'll ridicule me. God, where did that come from?

"No, I won't," she said. "You can do this."

Looking into her eyes, he almost believed her.

"You won't laugh?" he said.

"Of course not. Give it a shot."

"Hell." He reached for her hand and she automatically gave it. "I love the way you—" he swallowed back a ball forming in his throat "—appreciate my practical jokes, take care of me when I'm sick, cheer me up when I'm bummed."

Make me laugh out loud, accept me for who I am, give me completeness, fix my pipes. What the hell?

"She does all that?" Josie said.

"Who?"

"Simone?"

The name didn't register. He couldn't think past the vulnerable golden eyes staring back at him.

"Simone, right," he said, not knowing what else to do.

She broke eye contact and glanced at the fire.

With his forefinger and thumb, he guided her eyes back to his. "Should I say more?"

"No…you've said enough."

"Now, what?" His heart raced in anticipation, his hands crept up her arms and cradled her shoulders.

"I guess you're done—" she hesitated "—unless you want to…kiss her." Her tongue peeked out to wet her lower lip.

His pulse quickened. Practice. It was just practice. Getting the timing right, getting it perfect. Making himself into the perfect man to lure the perfect woman to the altar.

He leaned forward and brushed his lips against hers. A hint of marshmallow seasoned her sweet, soft lips, lips that naturally parted for him.

Was that the sound of J.B. galloping toward them, or Brett's heart pounding against his chest? He'd never felt this before when kissing Simone.

Simone. Simone. No. He wasn't kissing Simone. He was kissing...

"Mmm," Josie moaned, leaning into him.

He held her snugly against his body, pulling her closer.

Her scent tickled his nostrils; her flavor, all sweetness and innocence, drew him in. Somewhere in the back of his mind the voice of reason fought with his overactive hormones. But the voice was drowned out by the incredible ache in his chest. An ache for the woman he held in his arms.

She dug her fingers into his chest as she clung to his undershirt. He shifted her onto his lap, the evidence of his desire pressing against her thigh. She couldn't mistake it, couldn't mistake the need screeching from every pore of his body. Need for the woman of his dreams, the woman he'd waited a lifetime for...Josie.

No!

He broke the kiss, his mind pickled in confusion, his body aching in places he dared not admit. She slowly opened her eyes, looking at him with such trust, such wanting. Then reality shuttered her expression and her fingers sprung free of his shirt as if she'd been shocked.

"Good, good. Good kissing." She jumped to her

feet. "You did everything right today. A plus." She ran her fingers through her hair, hair he still found himself wanting to touch.

"Josie, I—"

"Did you see my headband? I know I brought it with me." She swiped her denim jacket from the bench beside the fire and dug through the pockets. "Even surprised myself today. I'm not a bad love teacher after all."

She slid the bright red band in place and he wanted to rip it from her hair. He liked her hair wild and free.

"Yep, think I'll place an ad in the *Herald*. 'Love lessons. Experienced teacher will share the secrets of romance.'" She shoved the candy, ham roll-ups and napkins into the backpack and zipped it up.

"What are you doing?" he said.

"Packing up. We're done. Lessons learned. We covered a lot of ground today and we weren't even planning on doing this—lessons, I mean." She took a deep breath and scanned the campsite. "What a gorgeous day. Let's ride some more. You know your way around these woods?"

"What about your ankle, your hip?" he said.

"I'm tough, remember?"

That's not all he remembered. She'd loved a man, lost him and would never love again. Josie deserved better.

"We didn't eat lunch," he said.

"Are you kidding? A piece of marshmallow fluff can last me six hours. Sticks to your ribs, know what I mean?"

No, he hadn't a clue what she was rambling about. He still struggled to see straight.

"Fresh air, horse dung, wet leaves," she continued.

"Truly a perfect day." She limped in the direction of the horses.

"You need help?" he offered, not standing for fear his arousal would embarrass him further.

"No, thanks. Just a strain," she said as she continued her brisk hobble out of sight. "Put the fire out, will ya?" she called over her shoulder.

Put the fire out. How in the hell was he going to do that when it was burning from the inside out?

Chapter Nine

It was the longest car ride of his life. Josie babbled about the weather until Brett finally turned up the radio, signaling his need for peace and quiet.

Hell, he needed to think.

But thirty minutes later he still hadn't made sense of the strange feelings burning his gut. Feelings he'd never felt before, with any woman.

It was a friendship like no other. A powerful bond between two people who thrived at being loners.

He never would have guessed how alone Josie was. She shouldn't be alone. She was a people person, a lighthearted, good-natured…widow. A widow who didn't date because she'd had her "one and only," her perfect husband, and Brett guessed no one could ever replace him. Especially not a man like Brett, who needed damn love lessons to get a woman to say "I do."

What in tarnation was he thinking about now? He

and Jo were neighbors, bowling partners, for crying out loud. Nothing more.

Then why couldn't he shake the taste of her from his lips? His insides were scrambled like a thousand-piece puzzle dumped to the floor. Everything in the wrong place, missing, hidden.

Thank God they were only minutes from home, where he'd find sanctuary in his apartment. The building he and Josie shared.

His fingers gripped the steering wheel.

"Hey, thanks again," she said.

"My pleasure." He kept his eyes trained to the road.

"Your friend J.B. is really nice. I got his number in case I want to go out to the farm by myself sometime."

He didn't know what irked him more: that J.B. was hitting on her, or that she was already planning for Brett's absence from her life once he married Simone.

"I guess you could do worse, dating-wise," Brett said.

"I told you, I don't date."

"Good thing. I can't stand the thought of you being pawed at by some jerk."

"My, aren't we protective," she said with that full-cheeked smile.

She didn't seem angry about it. That was a change.

"I can't help it. It's my job." At least for the next few days until he proposed to Simone.

"I'm really getting my taxes worth, Detective," she said.

This had nothing to do with his job as a public servant and everything to do with his feelings for Josie. Pulling onto Beverly Street, he struggled not to ask the next question. He lost.

"Your husband, Danny, he was that perfect?"

She glanced out the passenger window. "Nobody's perfect, Brett."

"Then why haven't you dated?" He slowed the truck to a crawl, not wanting her to hop out before they finished the conversation.

"You could say I had a chip of my own to knock off my shoulder. That, and the pain, kept me from looking again," she said.

"Don't you miss the closeness, the physical part?"

A strange sound came from her throat, like a hitched laugh. But she wasn't smiling.

"I miss the companionship and sense of belonging. The physical part was, well, let's just say I was naive when we married. But that wasn't the most important part. I mean, who wouldn't want a girl who worshipped you and planned her life around you? I did everything in my power to make him happy, but I don't think you'd call me a prodigy in bed. I'm not exactly a seductress."

No, but she was cute and playful, desirable in an innocent, natural way. Damn, how could she doubt her sexuality?

"Josie—"

"Can we not talk about this anymore?"

Turning into the lot, he pulled into his usual parking place, the one he and Josie fought for. The streetlights reflected off the blacktop, lighting her face.

"Oh, I almost forgot," she said, reaching into her jeans pocket. "The ring came off. Probably because of the cold."

Not making eye contact, she dropped it in his outstretched palm. He closed his fingers around the cool, white-gold band. A chill raced down his spine.

"Do you need help bringing stuff in?" she asked, not taking her eyes off his hand.

"I can manage."

It felt wrong, the ring in his hand, her hoarse voice, his pounding heart. He should slip the ring into his pocket, but couldn't move.

"Thanks. I had a great time," she said.

She glanced into his eyes and his breath caught. Had he caused the pain he saw there?

"Josie…" He touched the back of her hand that rested on the seat.

There was a moment's hesitation before she snatched it back, swung open the door and hopped out. "We got a lot done today. We can take tomorrow off."

Before he could respond, she raced up the sidewalk into the main door of their building, disappearing so fast he hardly believed they'd been together at all.

But they had been together, and not just as neighbors. She'd shared more of herself this afternoon than she had in the past two years, and he knew that wasn't easy for a woman like Jo.

She did it for him. To show him how to be generous with his feelings, to make him feel safe by exposing her darkest secrets and deepest fears. Didn't she just confess her insecurities as a woman? That must have cost her.

What could he do for her in return? There had to be something. He locked the truck and headed to his place.

Time for a night out. That's it. He'd show her what a special, attractive and amazing woman she was.

First, he'd buy her a gift, maybe some perfume or a scarf, something that showed her a man could, in fact, see her that way. That *he* saw her that way.

Formulating his plan, he opened his apartment door. It seemed colder than usual. He pulled the ring from his pocket and placed it on the breakfast bar. It didn't sparkle like he remembered, like when it hugged Josie's finger.

The ringing phone jarred him from his thoughts. He grabbed the receiver.

"Yeah?" he said, staring at the ring.

"Yeah? Yo? Boy, a few weeks away from me and you sound like a factory worker."

"Hi, Simone." He picked up the ring and took it to his bedroom, placing it safely in the velvet box.

"Where have you been? I called work and they said you took the day off," she said.

"I went riding at my friend's farm."

"By yourself?"

He hesitated. "Yeah."

How could he explain the afternoon spent with Josie when he didn't understand it himself?

"Save some time off for me, big guy."

"Don't worry, I've got plenty of days."

"Good, because I might fly in early, isn't that great?"

His gut clench tightened. "How early?"

"The day after tomorrow. I can't wait to see you."

"Me, too."

"Brett? You don't sound happy."

"I'm just thinking of everything I have to do before you get here."

"Like stocking up on whipped cream?" she teased.

His body normally would have stirred at the inference. He felt nothing.

"I'll be ready," he said.

"You'd better be. Gotta run. My other line's ringing. See you Saturday, Callahan. Oh, I love saying that." She smacked a kiss into the phone.

"Bye." He hung up.

He should be nervous about her imminent arrival, but he wasn't. Ambling to the couch, he grabbed the remote, not punching the power button. He'd better alert Jo. And tell her what? That he needed a crash course in love? That she had forty-eight hours to do the impossible?

He tapped the remote control to his knee. She deserved tonight off, time to recover from the afternoon of exposing her soul.

He still couldn't believe she'd done it. It took a lot of courage. He was too much of a coward to bare his insides to anyone. There was that spontaneous outburst at the beach when he'd described his loser parents. But that was a measly few sentences.

Since he'd taken tomorrow off, he'd have plenty of time to pick up something nice for Josie as a thank-you gift. More like a bribe. He'd better make it something better than a scarf. Maybe a dress?

He could be generous with his money, if not with his emotions.

He'd call her and plan a date. He'd buy some kind of frilly dress and have it delivered for their last night together, his graduation night.

In the meantime, he'd beg her to spend time with him tomorrow and share more secrets to make Simone say yes.

He was so very close to attaining the perfect wife.

He felt he was closing in on something big. With Jo's help, he'd have it all come Saturday.

She'd managed to avoid him most of the next day, and that was no easy feat. Calling, knocking, calling again, the man was a pitbull when determined to get his way. He wanted more time with Josie, more lessons to round out his rough spots.

First he showed up with doughnuts and fresh coffee at seven. She looked like hell, but he didn't seem to notice. Why would he? He saw her as nothing more than his buddy who could beat him at video games any day of the week.

As she ran her hands through her bed-head hairstyle, he'd rambled about needing to finish the lessons today. She shoved him into the hallway, told him *she* needed another few hours of sleep and shut the door in his face.

At eleven a bouquet of carnations arrived, her favorite. She called to thank him and nearly jumped out of her skin when he banged on the sliding door of her balcony. She flung open the door, thanked him properly, and told him to go home. She had work to do today. Real work. Then she locked the door and shut the drapes.

That didn't stop him from tapping. When it stopped a half hour later, she got suspicious and checked the balcony. He'd left another gift: a bag of Double Stuf Oreos. She was charmed. She read the note and understood his sudden desperation: Simone was coming tomorrow, not next week. He needed Jo. Now.

How she wished he needed her as more than a love tutor.

"Knock it off, Matthews," she scolded. He'd never

see her that way, especially after her confession of being a mediocre lover. She still couldn't believe she'd said it. Maybe it was for the best. It would keep things in perspective.

Her perspective was blown all to hell yesterday when he'd kissed her.

"All part of the curriculum," she said, digging through the box of goodies Wendy had sent her. She pulled out a tube of Lustrous Lip Gloss and read the fine print: Heat activated, use only as directed. Use generously to set fire to your lover's lips, or other erogenous spots.

"Oh, my," she said, taking off the cap. One thing for sure, Jo and Brett didn't need anything to set fire to their lips yesterday. She ran her tongue across her bottom lip remembering the hot, yet gentle kiss. A kiss so intense she'd drowned in the amazing sensations. When he broke the kiss and she'd opened her eyes, it took her a minute to figure out where she was and who she'd been kissing.

But Brett knew. He knew it was wrong and had stopped things before they got out of hand.

Which was one more reason she couldn't see him today: plain and simple embarrassment. She'd practically wrapped herself around the man out there in the woods. Her body lit in places she didn't think existed, heat pooled in other, more intimate places. Good God.

He'd probably put it all together by now. She'd gone without sex for five years, needed a quick fix and Brett was handy. Yesterday's kiss was a mistake, nothing more.

Then why did it feel so wonderful?

She closed her eyes and dug her fingernails into

her oak desk. It couldn't be. She couldn't be falling for the guy.

Face it, she couldn't be with Brett, but maybe it was time to let nature take its course and get out there into the dating game. This was the first time she'd considered seriously dating in years. That was a good sign. A sign she was finally healing.

Thanks to Brett.

It suddenly hit her why she'd never let any man get close. She was already close to Brett. His friendship had helped her heal in ways she couldn't have imagined, and she hadn't even realized it.

A knock echoed from the balcony door in the living room. She hated when he hooked a rope to her balcony and hoisted himself up. She thought for sure he'd break his neck one of these days.

Knock. Knock. Knock.

"Go away!" she shouted.

Focusing on the computer screen, she let her fingers fly across the keyboard. She had to concentrate on writing hot copy to go with Nadine's adult toys. At least if she couldn't have sex she should be able to enjoy writing about it.

Rub this electrifying gel onto your lover's...

Knock. Knock.

Bang! Bang!

"Argh! I can't work like this!" she cried.

"Josie!" Brett's muffled voice called. "Open up, I need—aaahhh!"

Something banged against the sliding door, then silence. Good grief, had he fallen off her balcony?

Racing through her apartment, she stubbed her toe on a ten-pound hand weight. Since when did she leave things scattered around? She whipped open the sliding door to an empty balcony. Panic gripped her stomach.

"Brett?" She leaned over the rail. Her heart pounded, her mouth went dry.

A hand reached up and grabbed her ankle.

"Gotcha!" He winked, swinging himself up and over the balcony railing.

"You jerk." She shoved at him with both hands.

"What?"

"Do you think that's funny? Pretending to be hurt? I thought you'd finally fallen on your butt and broken your neck."

"I had to get you to open the door," he said, all innocence.

"Go home." She turned to go back inside, but he grabbed her wrist.

"Josie?"

She gritted her teeth. When he called her by her full nickname her insides melted. "What?"

"I need you."

And I need you. She closed her eyes. It was too late. She'd fallen in love with the jerk.

"I'm sorry that I scared you, okay? But I'm desperate," he said.

Aren't we all?

"Fine, come inside," she said.

He let go of her wrist, but the warmth of his touch continued to crawl up her arm and settle across her shoulders. If she really cared about him, the least she could do was help him get what he really wanted: Simone.

"I'll be right back." She ambled into the bedroom and grabbed her love notes. Taking a deep breath, she swallowed back the lump rising in her chest. She rejoined Brett in the living room. He was talking to Fred.

"Women. Can't please 'em no matter what you do," he said to the reptile. "It's not like I'm a complete loser. I know which fork to use on the salad, and I don't belch in public."

Standing in the doorway, she cleared her throat.

"I'm ready." He rubbed his hands together.

She started toward the couch.

"Here, let me." He adjusted a few pillows behind her back as she sat down. His hand grazed her lower back and a heaviness settled down low. She wanted this over.

"Oreos?" he offered, grabbing the bag from the table.

"No, thanks."

"Come on, I'll feed them to you."

And she'd fall apart right here.

"Why are you being so solicitous?" she said.

"I know I'm asking a lot. You've got things to do. You've got your own life."

An empty life without love. An even emptier life once Brett married Simone and cut Josie from his world.

"Sit down over there." She pointed with her pen. He sat in the wing chair and gripped the arms.

"Relax," she said.

"I can't. I have to ask you something."

"No, I will not propose for you."

"Not funny." He fisted his hands in his lap, a very unusual gesture for him, as if he was struggling to keep hold of his emotions.

"Do you really think I have a chance with Simone?'' he asked, then glanced at the floor. Humility was one helluva sexy trait in a man.

"I mean," he continued, not looking at her, "what if I'm not good enough for her?"

"What are you talking about?" She couldn't believe he thought such a thing.

He stood and paced to the balcony. "Who am I fooling, Jo? I'm just a punk from the South Side. What have I got to offer someone like Simone?"

"Stop talking like that. You're a kind, loyal and generous friend. You're clever and funny. She'd be lucky to be your wife."

"I hope you're right."

Her heart broke. Truth was, he was too good for the princess.

"Let's move on, Detective. Okay, we've covered sentimental, compassionate, generous, macho, funny and mind-reading skills."

"What's left?"

"Being thoughtful, check. Flowers for no reason at all—" she glanced at the bouquet of carnations on her dining table "—check. Picking up after yourself. I'll inspect your apartment later."

He grimaced. "What else have you got on that list?"

"Two more: Kissing her and gently stroking her hair can go with holding her without expecting sex out of the deal."

"I'll never get that one."

"You held me yesterday, remember?"

"Yeah, but you're…" His voice trailed off.

Brett struggled to define what she was. She was more than a friend, much more.

"I know, I'm not Simone," she said.

"No, you're not." He saw a stranger sitting across the room. A stranger he had no trouble being generous with. He'd naturally offered her compassion, was generous to a fault, even read her mind at times. All things he struggled to master in his relationship with Simone.

"Yesterday was good practice," she said. "You held me and stroked my hair and had no desire to have sex."

Like hell he didn't. What was he thinking?

Her buzzer went off and she sprung from the sofa. "I think you've graduated, Detective. You'll sweep Simone off her feet."

For some reason her words didn't improve his mood.

She punched the intercom. "Yes?"

"Delivery from Annabelle's Boutique for Josie Matthews."

She hit the buzzer and turned to Brett. "I didn't order anything. I'll bet Wendy's behind this. She's desperate for that damned copy."

She flung open the door, signed for the delivery and raced to the sofa, package in hand. "What the heck?" She ripped open the box and fumbled through the tissue.

When she pulled out the dress, he knew he'd done good. Her eyes lit like a little girl opening her first Barbie doll on Christmas morning. She turned the dress this way and that, admiring the delicate lace that overlaid the peach-colored satin. Annabelle said it was a winner, feminine and sexy.

"Wow," she said. She spread it across the back of the sofa and just stared at it, framing her cheeks with her hands.

His heart skipped.

A minute later, she pulled out the card and read it silently, then glanced at him in confusion. "I don't get it."

"I thought we could go out tonight, as a thank-you celebration. I made reservations at The Wellington. Our last night together."

As he said the words, his heart burned as if he'd eaten five pounds of pepperoni.

"Thanks. That was sweet." She put the dress back in the box and covered it with tissue.

"You like it, don't you?" he said.

"It's beautiful."

"Then it's a date?"

"I can't." She pushed the box aside. "This isn't me. You know that. I'm not the fancy-dress type."

"I just thought we could celebrate in style. Go out to a nice restaurant."

"Oh, I get it. Practice for Simone."

"No, this has nothing to do with her."

"If you want to thank me, or celebrate, or whatever, just take me to Peeps for a hot dog."

"But I thought—"

"You can't change me, Brett. I am what I am. I'm not the fancy-dress type. I'm just Jo, one of the guys, remember?"

"I wasn't trying to change you." And she was anything but one of the guys, dressed in tight sweats and a midriff T-shirt. He tried keeping his eyes off her touchable band of exposed flesh.

"You've thanked me enough," she said. "The trip to the farm, the beach."

"You got hurt at the farm and I was pretending you were Simone at the beach."

"I still had fun." She chuckled. "You can tell I don't get out much."

He wanted to remedy that, but his hands were tied. Or rather, his heart was spoken for.

"I'm thinking that's going to change," she said.

"What's going to change?"

"My life. You've inspired me in many ways."

She sat down, stretched her arms out across the back of the sofa and crossed one leg over the other. An air of confidence sparkled in her eyes.

"I'm working on the first fairy-tale book again," she said. "And I've decided to pursue a social life outside of my little two-bedroom apartment. I've asked Wendy to help me."

Hell, not that lunatic. Brett didn't want Josie meeting anyone, especially not Wendy's seconds. Josie deserved a man who would cherish her and protect her. Not some one-night stand.

And not a man who wanted someone else.

"Go slow," he said.

"Yeah, I know. I'm not the most experienced woman around, so I'm an easy target. Don't worry, I might be mediocre in the sex department, but I do have a good head on my shoulders."

Mediocre? Was she nuts? He'd seen the way she went after things, with vengeance and determination. He'd bet his stock of frozen pizzas she was like that in bed. Ten times over. His body tightened at the thought.

"All I'm saying is, be careful." He clicked into big-brother mode, a safe place to be. "There are a lot of idiots out there."

"You care," she said with an open hand to her chest.

"Of course I care." He truly did, more than he should.

Truth was, he had a hard time seeing a life without Josie nagging him about sleep or fixing his leaky pipes. He couldn't imagine going a week, much less a lifetime without watching *The Year the Earth Stood Still* on her sofa, eating pizza with everything but pineapple.

He couldn't imagine life without her, period.

"Josie?" he said.

"Yes?"

"Would you at least try on the dress?"

"Is it really that important to you?"

"Yeah, it is."

"Okay." She picked up the box and disappeared into her bedroom.

He didn't know why he'd just asked her to put on the dress, other than that he was stalling for time. He feared once he left her place, that would be it. The end. There'd be no reason for them to see each other again.

Why should that matter? He was starting his new life with, hopefully, his fiancée. The woman of his dreams. He'd come so far in the last week, he'd learned so much. From Josie.

A fascinating girl who could rattle off baseball statistics one minute and melt your heart with a gentle kiss the next.

A horrible thought struck him: when she had kissed Brett, had she been imagining her husband kissing her? Her one and only true love?

He paced to the overstuffed chair and sat down. It killed him to think she'd been alone these past five years, grieving for the one man who could fill that empty spot in her heart.

Would Simone ever feel that way about Brett? More important, would Brett ever love Simone with that kind of intensity? He loved her, sure, in his own way. But that hole in his heart didn't close up when he thought about marrying her. Something was missing. He'd hoped Josie would help him figure it out.

"Well, here I am."

She walked into the living room, modeling the dress with a tentative spin. He stopped breathing, completely. She looked beautiful, like a princess, the low neck revealing the slight swell of her breasts. God help him, she looked perfect.

If she was let loose into the dating scene, she'd be eaten alive.

"We're going out. Now." He stood and took her hand. "Come downstairs and wait for me to change into a suit."

"You really don't have to do this," she said as he led her to the door.

"Oh, yes, I do. It's time I taught you a few things about men so you can defend yourself."

"Hey, just because I've only had one lover doesn't mean I'm helpless."

He wished she wouldn't refer to herself that way. "I know you're not helpless, Josie. But I'm not going to let you go out there without some practice. Tonight it's my turn to teach you."

Chapter Ten

The Wellington Restaurant was crowded, but Brett managed to get them an intimate table in the far corner of the restaurant.

"I'll have the roast beef and my date will have..." He glanced at Josie.

"Chicken à la Wellington, please."

"Soup or salad?" the waitress, a middle-aged brunette asked. "The soup is clam chowder."

"Salad with blue cheese," Josie said.

"Same here."

The waitress scribbled down their order. "Another glass of wine, ma'am?" she asked Jo, who was halfway into her first.

"She's fine," Brett said. "But I'll take another cola."

The waitress nodded, took their menus and walked away.

"Cutting me off at one glass, eh?" Josie said, raising her wineglass in a toast.

"When you go out with a strange man you want to keep a clear head."

"*Strange* being a relative term," she teased.

"I'm not goofing around here, Jo. You've been out of the game for too long to know how to handle yourself."

"Hey, I haven't spilled my wine or tripped the waitress yet."

"You know what I mean." He glanced at a table of businessmen. "Listen up. The trick is observing things very closely. Watching for odd behavior or inconsistencies."

"Are we talking about dating or police work?" she said.

"Both. Now, what would attract you to a man?"

"His teeth?"

"Be serious."

"His eyes, I guess, and his smile."

Great. She'd be suckered in by any guy with a decent smile. Well, that accounted for three-quarters of the male population.

"How would you judge whether or not he was safe?" he asked.

"The amount of hair gel he used?"

"Josie, I'm serious. First, never go anywhere alone the first time you meet someone. Stay in a public place. Don't even go for a walk alone. Got it?"

"Should I be taking notes?"

"I'll type it up in triplicate."

"Now, that I'd like to see," she said.

"Second, find out something about a guy before going anywhere with him. Call me and I'll do a background check."

"Yes, sir."

"Third. If a guy can't look you in the eye, dump him. Fourth, remember that if it sounds too good to be true, it probably is."

The waitress served their salads and Brett's cola.

"Okay, so if he says he's a millionaire and wants to make me his queen he's probably broke." She smiled.

"Are you taking me seriously?" He stabbed his salad.

"I said I was going to think about dating in the near future, not take out an ad in the personals. On second thought—" she hesitated, then picked up her fork "—that might not be such a bad idea."

"Fifth, no taking out personal ads and absolutely no blind dates."

"I pity your daughters."

"Why?" He sat back and put his fork on his plate.

"I'm cautious." *And worried as hell about you.*

"You're overprotective." She grabbed a roll.

He couldn't help it. It had become a habit with her.

"Let's practice," he said.

"You want me to pick up one of those guys?" She eyed the table of businessmen.

"Hell, no. There's no 'picking up' anybody."

She smiled at him. Damn, with that smile she wouldn't have to pick up anybody. They'd follow her home like lost puppies.

"Let's get clear on a few things," Brett said. "Your date offers to pay for dinner—"

"And I let him."

"No, you don't," he said.

"Why not?"

"He'll expect something in return."

"I assume I'd have to kiss him."

"What if he expects more?"

"I push him down the stairs?"

"Get some pepper spray. Now, what do you do if he says 'Your hair is so beautiful' and reaches out to touch it."

"Well, obviously he's lying so I dump him."

"Why do you say that? Your hair is beautiful." He reached out and fingered a few strands of spun gold, then brushed her cheek with the back of his knuckles.

"What do I do now?" she said.

His gaze locked onto her amber eyes. "About what?"

"About you touching my hair?"

"Does it bother you?" His pulse raced.

"No, but you're my…" Her voice trailed off.

What? What the hell was he to her, anyway? Friend? Neighbor? Soul mate?

"Roast beef," the waitress said, placing his plate in front of him.

He jerked his hand away from Josie's cheek and stared at his food in confusion.

The waitress served Josie her chicken. "Anything else?" she said.

How about a map to navigate his way out of this mess? He wanted Simone to love him; he wanted her to be his wife. He liked Josie and couldn't imagine life without her. But he didn't think Simone would understand him bringing Josie home for Monday night football. How had it gotten so damned complicated?

"I think we're okay," Josie said to the waitress.

Speak for yourself.

"So, tomorrow's the big day?" Josie asked.

He looked at her, this stranger who shared a booth

with him, and couldn't for the life of him figure out what she was talking about.

"Simone?" she prompted. "She's coming to Chicago tomorrow."

"I don't want to talk about it." Brett sat back in the booth and studied his meal.

Josie leaned toward him and touched the sleeve of his suit jacket. Why did his heart do a triple beat every time she touched him?

"You've learned a lot this week. You'll be fine, Brett," she said, sincerity in her eyes.

But deep down he knew he'd never be fine again, not without Josie.

"I could care less about getting Simone to love me," Brett said. "If she really loves me, she'll accept me for who I am."

"Bravo!" She clapped. "You've finally got it."

Not quite, but it was coming, and he didn't like what he saw. He was chasing a pipe dream when the woman he really wanted sat in the booth beside him.

No, this wasn't right for Josie. Even if the feeling was mutual he wouldn't do that to her, wouldn't saddle her with a man who was so insensitive that he couldn't see the obvious when it bit him in the butt.

His beeper cut him off. He ripped the damned thing from his belt. "It's Mulligan. I'd better call in."

"Make it quick. I want to order dessert."

"Be right back," he said.

He found the pay phone and tried to call in, but hit the wrong numbers. Confusion jumbled his brain. And fear. Fear that he'd screw up somehow and hurt Josie.

He couldn't do that.

On the third try he got the numbers right and Mulligan answered.

"It's me," Brett said. "What's up?"

"We need you to ID the Wallace kid."

"You got him in custody?"

"We're watching the house. Can you stop by?"

"Now?"

"He's here now. If you don't ID him we can't bring him in."

"Fine. I'm on my way."

He hung up and took a deep breath. Why now, when he had things to say to Josie? Important things, like maybe he'd made a mistake and didn't want Simone.

Then what the hell did he want? He couldn't play with Josie's feelings like that, couldn't drag her into the middle of his messed-up emotions.

He'd known exactly what he'd wanted at the start of this love-lesson course. What had changed?

His heart. He'd recognized something amazing and special. Something he'd never experienced before. Love?

He returned to the table with his best "I'm sorry" smile.

"Uh-oh, I know that look," she said.

"I gotta go in."

"No problem. I'll hang around and have dessert. You want me to bring you home something?" She eyed the dessert menu.

Brett glanced at one of the businessmen who kept looking in Josie's direction. He smiled a sinister, ugly smile.

"I think you should go home," Brett said.

"Why?"

"There're too many wolves around here, Josie."

"Don't worry, hero-cop. I can take care of myself. Besides, you won't be around much longer to protect me."

Her words were like a knife slicing through his chest. He wouldn't be around to taunt her, tickle her and make her smile that amazing smile of hers. He'd never hear that giggle, or beat her at checkers or—

"Go on, I'll be fine," she said. "I really want to have dessert."

"Okay, here." He dropped two fifty-dollar bills on the table. "I expect change."

"Yes, sir," she teased.

He leaned forward and gave her a kiss on the cheek. "Be careful."

"Now, that's funny coming from a cop."

"Did you get anything out of what I said tonight?"

"Sure, guys lie to get what they want."

His gut constricted. She was right. He'd been lying to himself. But he hadn't wanted anything from her at the start of this other than help in the romance department. Who would have thought his plan would backfire?

He glanced one more time at the businessmen, not wanting to leave her alone. She was determined to satisfy that sweet tooth of hers.

"Kiss me," he said to her. "And make it good."

"What?"

"Just do it. To keep those guys off your back."

Who was he kidding?

He gently pulled her to her feet and kissed her hard, claiming his territory for all the world to see. But when the kiss turned warm and gentle he busted apart inside. She moaned against his lips and he held her closer, wanting more. This was so easy, so right.

Breaking the kiss, he took a deep breath and struggled to remember why he'd kissed her, and why he'd stopped.

In truth, he wanted her like nobody's business and it scared the hell out of him. This was Jo. He couldn't mess with her like this.

"I need to go," he said, his voice hoarse.

"I know." She blinked those amazing eyes.

He gently guided her back to the booth. But instead of turning to leave, he stood there and stared at her. He couldn't keep denying it. What he had with Josie was more than friendship. Much more.

"I don't understand," he blurted out.

"I know." She smiled, as if she knew exactly what was happening.

"I have to go," he said, his lips still tingling from the kiss.

"Call me later?"

"If I'm late I'll stop by in the morning. I'll bring doughnuts." He paused. "And Oreos."

"Not too early. I need my beauty rest."

"Sweetheart, you couldn't be more beautiful if you tried." He ran his thumb across her lips, turned and escaped before he did something stupid like get arrested for performing a lewd act in public.

Walking toward the exit, he paused and glanced over his shoulder. Yeah, it was really Josie sitting there, pretty as the girl next door, a twinkle in her eye, a smile playing at the corner of her lips.

In that split second, he could have sworn he read her thoughts.

I love you.

He raced to the car and started for the Wallace house. Josie loved him. He knew this deep down in his soul. It felt comfortable and right and he didn't even have to jump through hoops to make it happen.

Too bad. He wasn't the right man for her, not by a long shot. She needed someone giving and compassionate, and all the other things on that love-lessons list of hers. Sure, she said he'd mastered them all, but he doubted it.

Brett suspected her husband had mastered every lesson and swept her off her feet into the perfect life. He could never compete with that. Nor should he want to. She had done so much for him, sacrificed her time and emotions.

He had to think of her first, of what was the right thing for Josie.

As his brain kicked into high gear, he drove down Algonquin Street hoping that the Wallace kid would show his face quickly and Brett could refocus on what to do next about Josie.

What to do next? That should be a no-brainer. Stick to plan A, marry the perfect woman and leave Josie to find happiness with a better man.

He gripped the steering wheel with deadly force. If Brett was any kind of "better" man, he'd let Josie go and walk away. But could he?

The next morning, Josie soaked in a hot bath, reliving last night in her mind. She couldn't have mistaken their kiss. It claimed her like nothing else had.

And with that kiss came the realization that she'd fallen in love with her best friend.

It felt so right.

She didn't have to act a certain way around Brett.

She was who she was, and he accepted her for it. She didn't even mind him doing things for her. When he offered his help it didn't feel overpowering or controlling. He did it because he cared about her. But how much did he care?

She'd been disappointed when he hadn't called last night. He probably got home in the wee hours and didn't want to wake her. As if she could sleep?

Swirling bubbles with her toes, she contemplated what she'd say to him, how she'd tell him they were meant to be together. She'd better have a brick handy just in case.

But she knew he'd get it eventually, like she did. It amazed her how he appreciated those qualities that made her different from Simone the Socialite. She didn't have to pretend with Brett or worry about impressing him.

The funny thing was, she knew they'd be amazing in bed. She wanted him in a way she'd never felt before. They'd be so anxious to please each other and would accept each other unconditionally. There'd be no room for insecurities.

Mercy, she loved so many things about the man, especially his tender heart and sense of humor.

Someone knocked at the door. Brett?

"Just a minute," she called.

She climbed out of the tub and put on her terrycloth robe, tying it in front. She felt different today, sexy. To think she'd lived without feeling sexy for years. She smiled. That had changed, thanks to Brett.

Peering through the peephole, she saw Wendy pacing the hall. Her friend had called earlier looking for Nadine's copy. Josie opened the door. "You're a slave driver, anyone ever tell you that?"

"Hello to you, too." Wendy brushed past her into the living room. "This isn't about Nadine's copy."

"What, then?"

She eyed her. "I was worried. You sounded funny on the phone this morning, and the fact you asked about getting your nails done was a sure sign you were on the verge of a breakdown."

"Hey, I resent that remark." She ambled to the sofa and sat down, tucking her legs beneath her.

"Resent it all you like." Her friend sat on the coffee table. "What gives?"

She gazed across the room and out the sliding glass door. Brett gives. He gives love, compassion, tenderness.

Wendy snapped her fingers in Josie's face.

"Earth to Josie." She leaned forward, her eyes squinting. "Oh, my God. I know that look. But there isn't anyone in your life, you don't date and have no contact with men except for your clients and…the detective. You slept with the detective?"

Josie grinned. "We didn't sleep together. But I think he finally gets it."

"Gets what?"

"That we're more than friends."

"I knew it!" She jumped to her feet and clapped her hands together. "Your friendship was a front. Here you thought I was being a jerk when I jumped on top of him."

"You were being a jerk."

"I was trying to move things along. You're welcome."

She winked, but Josie didn't miss the tinge of melancholy in her eyes. For all of Wendy's conquests, Jo suspected she really craved one special man to love.

"Unbelievable," Wendy whispered. "Here you get the Incredible Hunk and I have to break a blind date to work overtime."

"Bummer."

"New client. Very demanding. So, when do you see him next?"

"Not sure. He worked last night so I suspect he's sleeping it off. I wish I was down there with him." She couldn't help but grin.

Wendy grinned right along with her, then spent the next half hour giving her a refresher course on makeup. Josie kept telling her she didn't need to dolly herself up for Brett, that he loved her the way she was. But Wendy wasn't having any of it.

Once Wendy left, Josie got dressed in her tightest jeans and a snug flower-power T-shirt. Admiring herself in a dresser mirror, she said, "What a difference a week makes."

She felt confident and feminine, and a little bit...sexy. She decided she liked the feeling.

Someone knocked at the door. This time it had to be Brett. Her cheeks warmed.

Instead, through the peephole she eyed her neighbor, Katy, standing in the hallway. Josie opened her door.

"Katy?"

The woman's fingers trembled as she gripped a gingham dish towel. "How is he?"

"Who?"

"You don't know? I'm sorry."

"What?"

"My sister, the nurse, called this morning. We talked about Detective Callahan, how good he is to

Kelsey and Kortney. She said he was brought in this morning."

The world tipped on its axis, and Josie struggled to breathe. "Brought in?"

"Something happened at work, he was unconscious when they brought him in." The woman grabbed Josie's hand for support. "I thought for sure you knew since you were such good friends."

Were. Past tense. Panic swirled in her belly.

"No," was all Josie could say, her mind a jumble of emotions. "Which hospital?"

"Holy Family."

In a daze, Josie grabbed her jacket off the coatrack and rattled the pocket to make sure she had her keys.

"Can you drive?" Katy asked.

"I'll be fine." In truth she wasn't sure if she'd ever be fine again.

Racing down the stairs to her car, she struggled to keep a lid on her emotions so she could drive. She had to get to him, had to make sure he was okay.

Getting in the car, she gripped the steering wheel until her knuckles turned white. What if he wasn't okay?

"That isn't an option." She gritted her teeth and drove to the hospital, five miles over the speed limit. She was a master of control after years of keeping her needs in check and more years pretending to be satisfied living alone.

She didn't know how unsatisfied she was until Brett walked into her life.

Hurt. Brett was hurt. Unconscious. She'd just found him and now was about to lose him. Not fair. Being alone again after finding completeness.

Familiar feelings flowed through her body. Anger,

remorse, devastation. She'd been married to Danny for too short a time when fate took him away, and now she'd finally recovered, she'd found peace in another man's arms.

Brett. He'd helped her heal and now was being taken away from her.

No. She couldn't survive another loss like this.

She found a spot in the hospital parking lot and sprinted into the emergency room. As she hovered beside the nurse's desk, background noises buzzed in her ears: ringing phones, the waiting-room television, voices drifting from down the hall.

The nurse finished her phone call and looked at Josie.

"I'm looking for a patient named Brett Callahan," Josie said.

She checked the computer screen. "He's been moved to room 311."

Josie absently followed the signs on the walls, leading her to Brett. He'd be okay. He had to be okay.

What if he wasn't? What if he died, like Danny, leaving a gaping hole in her heart?

She spotted a doctor coming out of his room. "How is he?" she asked.

"And you are?"

"His neighbor." *His soul mate.*

"He's got some cracked ribs, a few stitches in his right arm, minor abrasions. He was in a lot of pain so we gave him a sedative."

"But he's okay, right?"

"Okay as he can be considering he was hit by a car. If you'll excuse me." He stuck his pen in his lab coat and walked away.

She took a deep breath and pushed open the door.

Her breath caught at the sight of him: a goose egg swelled above his right eye; an IV stuck out from his hand; and a white bandage covered his forearm. He looked so weak and broken. Nothing like the man she'd fallen in love with.

"Who are you?" A woman asked accusingly as she came out of the bathroom. She scooted a chair to Brett's bedside and possessively took his hand and Josie knew the woman was Simone.

"I'm his neighbor."

"Did you bring his things?"

"Excuse me?"

"I asked my assistant to contact a neighbor and get some of Brett's things. I assume that's why you're here."

"No, I...I heard what happened and wanted to make sure he was okay."

Simone eyed Josie from head to toe, then turned back to Brett. "It's horrible. He shouldn't have to risk his life."

"What happened?"

"I don't know the details, and frankly, I don't care. I can't stand seeing him like this."

Josie knew the feeling.

"But we'll fix everything, won't we, sweetheart?" Simone kissed his hand. "Daddy is going to finance his security business. We'll get him out of this dangerous line of work, no matter what he says."

It hit Josie like a gust of sub-zero wind: Simone was truly the right woman for Brett. She was strong and supportive and didn't run at the first sign of trouble. All that and she had the ability to get him out of police work and keep him safe.

She was here, taking care of him, giving him everything he'd always wanted, everything he needed.

Unlike Josie, who crumbled at the first sign of adversity. The very sight of him so still and broken made her want to flee the state.

Loving Brett was not enough. She had to do the right thing and let him go, push him into the arms of the woman who'd be there when he needed her most.

That woman was not Josie.

"I'm glad you're here with him," she said to Simone.

"I got to town early and was going to surprise him. The woman at the police station said they'd brought him here."

"He looks so…" Josie's voice trailed off.

Simone straightened her shoulders. "He'll be better soon, won't you, hero-cop?"

He didn't answer. He just lay there, unconscious, breathing in and out…in and out.

Simone turned and looked at Josie. "I'll tell him you came by, Miss…?"

"That's okay. I'll call tomorrow." She ambled to his bedside, touched his hand and choked down a sob.

You'll be okay, Brett. Everything will be okay.

She smiled at Simone and escaped the hospital as fast as she could. Only when she got to the parking lot did a sob escape her throat. She bit back the tears, tears of loss and regret. No, not regret. She'd never regret the time they'd spent together. Nothing could take that away from them.

She'd loved like never before. She'd taught him what he needed to be the perfect male, and he'd shown her she didn't have to be alone. Now he could go on to love a strong woman who'd give him everything he'd ever wanted.

Pulling the station wagon out of the lot, she planned the next few days. She'd leave him a note, then pack up and head north to Wisconsin. She always did her best thinking, her best healing by the lake at Shorewood. This was going to take a lot of time to heal.

Who was she kidding? Brett Callahan was one man she'd never recover from.

Chapter Eleven

It was quiet up north, so very quiet. Josie sat on the front porch step of her rented cabin and sipped her root beer. This had always been the perfect place for thinking, close enough to the lake to hear the waves splash against the shore, far enough away from civilization.

After Danny's death, she'd spent plenty of time here, recovering, planning, figuring out what to do next. She wasn't sure how she'd go on.

She thought she'd be safe in a suburb of Chicago, in her new life with no ties to anyone. The ache in her chest proved otherwise.

It had all happened so quickly. One minute she was helping Brett with his love skills, the next, she'd fallen in love herself. How did she miss the signs?

It didn't matter. By now he'd have read her note and would be grateful for her quick exit from his life. After all, his goal had been to snag the perfect wife.

Perfect didn't describe Josie at present. There was

a snag in her purple sweater, a hole in the knee of her jeans and her hair was a mess, as usual.

Brett had never minded her wild hair. He hadn't minded a lot of things: her need for order; her talent fixing drain pipes; her wacky sense of fashion.

She stood and stretched her legs. "Time for a walk."

Following the long, sandy trail toward the shore, she paused to admire the fall colors adorning the trees. It was peaceful out here, the smell of fresh earth, the sound of the lake.

Only, something was missing. Someone to share the experience, the man she loved.

"This is pathetic," she whispered, kicking at a tree branch in her path.

Pathetic, maybe, but it wasn't going away. She couldn't stop loving Brett any more than she could have prevented the anguish that consumed her after Danny's death. Hundreds of miles didn't do it. A new life didn't do it. She continued to drown in the pain. Pain of losing Danny, of losing her life.

Voices echoed from the path below and she panicked. This was a choice getaway spot for folks from her hometown of Keller, thirty miles away. She crouched behind a fallen tree and held her breath.

The voices got louder. A man and woman's voice accompanied by the giggles of children. The sound touched her heart. She closed her eyes.

As the voices drifted past, she stood and peered through the brush. That was close.

Close to what? Seeing people who would remind her of her past? She'd healed and moved on, finally, after five years. It wasn't as if seeing old friends would open the old wounds.

No, she'd been cowering for another reason.

She raced down the path right up to the shore. The water creeped up the sand to touch the toes of her sneakers. With trembling fingers, she framed her face in her hands.

Embarrassment. That was it. She was embarrassed to be seen because people from her hometown would recognize her for what she was, a coward. Only a coward would have run five years ago instead of coming home to work through her grief with people who loved her. She should have stood up to her family, told them she appreciated their love, but needed to stand on her own for a change.

Shame bubbled up inside. As she stared at the angry waves of Lake Michigan, it struck her that no matter how far she ran, life would find her. Pain would find her. She'd run from Danny's death, pain her constant partner, and now she'd run from Brett. It did no good. Her heart still ached for the man she loved.

The love she felt for Brett wouldn't stop because he was out of her life, because she'd thrown him into the arms of another woman.

"Rats," she said, hugging her ribs. All her planning and micromanaging was useless. She had little control over life; she didn't mean to fall in love with Brett.

Life had thrown her curveballs, and instead of stepping up to the plate and hitting them, she ran, just like she was running now.

She was sick of running.

It was time for her to grow up and face life head-on, embrace the unknown. After all, anything could happen at any time. Danny had had a safe job and still died a young man. There were no guarantees. Although she could pretty much guarantee she'd never stop loving Brett.

Why should she? They laughed, teased and shared the most intimate details of their lives. Their relationship was a gift from God. She had no right to turn her back on it.

"Time to go home." She made the climb to the cabin, hoping it wasn't too late, hoping he hadn't already proposed to Simone.

"I won't accept that." Simone was all wrong for him, a mirage that disappeared when you got too close. He wouldn't be happy with a materialistic, high-society girl. Brett needed someone down-to-earth and playful.

He needed Josie.

She shoved T-shirts, jeans and multicolored socks into her backpack.

She was through running and being scared. She loved Brett and was going to tell him so. She didn't care that Simone was perfect. Perfection was an illusion. Love wasn't.

Brett couldn't believe she'd abandoned him, didn't visit him in the hospital, didn't stop by when he got home. Had he dreamed it all? Had he imagined the sparkle of love in her eyes? The incredible connection he had to a remarkable woman?

"More coffee?" Simone asked from his kitchen.

"No, thanks," he said as politely as possible. It was a struggle. He wanted to be alone. He wanted Josie more.

He closed his eyes and relaxed against the cushions of the leather couch. He didn't think the nightmare could have gotten any worse. A drug lead gone wrong was bad enough, but then to lose Josie...that was the worst part.

The words in her note stung his heart.

You need a strong woman, a woman like Simone. You were right all along. Trust your instincts.

His instincts were telling him Simone couldn't be more wrong for Brett.

And Josie couldn't be more right.

But she was gone, on vacation, according to his neighbor, Katy. Like hell. She was running. From him. The thought drove him insane as he went over the last few days, the last few years in his mind. She'd run because she couldn't stand the pain. She'd been running ever since her husband died, burying herself in work and the anonymity of living in a new town, creating a new life.

He thought better of her than that. He thought her a fighter. How could he have been so wrong?

"I bought pastries from a local bakery," Simone said, walking into the living room.

Those spiked heels combined with the apron she'd picked up at the Kitchen Kart in town made for a surreal combination. He would have chuckled if his chest didn't hurt so damned much.

"Here." She sat down and held out a pastry for him to sample.

"I'm really not—"

She shoved it into his mouth.

He chewed, swallowed hard and forced a smile. "Great, thanks."

"I'm glad they're managing at work so I could be here for you. Maybe in a few days you'll be up to tasting other things besides pastry?'' The gleam in her eye made him uneasy.

The truth was he'd tasted real love. Now nothing else would do.

''Simone, we need to talk.''

''After I put more pastries on a plate.'' She started for the kitchen.

''Enough with the pastries,'' he snapped.

She turned, her lower lip curled into a full pout.

''Sorry. This is important.''

She pulled a dining room chair next to the couch and sat, crossing one leg over the other.

''You and me...'' he started.

Her eyes sparkled.

What a horrible thing to have to do.

''I really appreciate everything you've done for me these last few days. Feeding me, getting my mail, answering my phone. I couldn't have done it without you.''

She beamed.

''You're perfect, Simone. Truly perfect.'' He looked into her eyes and took a deep breath. ''You're just not perfect for me.''

Her eyes widened for a split second, then her brows crinkled in confusion. ''What are you talking about?''

''You, me, marriage.''

''Marriage?''

''Yeah, you know, honor, obey, all that stuff.''

She stood and brushed her palms on her apron. ''I don't know where you got the idea I was interested in you as a husband. I just know a good business investment when I see one.'' She ambled to the breakfast bar.

Good save, he thought. Lucky for him she was being polite. He wasn't sure he could deal with her pain. He had enough trouble dealing with his own.

"I've got all the paperwork in order, a list of businesses for you to solicit," she said. "I hope you take Daddy and me up on our offer. You're a natural businessman."

She poured herself another cup of coffee and he noticed her hands tremble. Damn. He felt bad, really bad. He didn't want to hurt her. But he couldn't lie anymore, especially to himself.

Simone fiddled with the stack of mail, and he could tell she wanted out of here more than a cougar wanted out of a cage.

"You've had a rough couple of days taking care of me," he said. "Why don't you take off?"

"Well, I do have some calls to make from our Chicago office. You can always page me if you need anything. I'll be in town for a few weeks." She placed the apron on the bar stool.

Tossing her full-length coat over her arm, she grabbed her purse and made one last cursory scan of the room, as if it would be her last. They both knew this to be true.

"Take care," she said.

"You, too." He wanted to say more. He couldn't.

She padded to the door, then hesitated but didn't turn around. "She's nice."

"Who?" he said.

"The one who came to see you at the hospital. She's sweet. You'll be happy."

His heart ached. If only that were true.

"Simone?"

She turned, tipping her chin up as she looked at him.

"Thank you," he said. "For everything."

A loud knock interrupted the moment and Simone opened the door. Brett's heart slammed against his chest at the sight of Josie standing in the doorway.

"Josie?"

She ignored him and squared off at Simone. "I know you may be perfect, but I love him. He's the most generous, caring, funny, sensitive man I know and I'm not going to give him up without a fight. I'm done being afraid. I don't care if he's a cop or a cook. I want that man over there," Josie rambled.

His heart soared.

Simone stood there, a dumbfounded look on her face.

"Miss…"

"Matthews." Josie crossed her arms over her chest.

"Miss Matthews, yes, well, I believe there's been a misunderstanding. My father is known for investing in small businesses and I think Brett's security venture is perfect for Trifarra Inc. That's where our relationship ends. There's nothing personal going on here."

"Oh," Josie said, her cheeks flushing pink.

Simone glanced over her shoulder. "Goodbye, Brett."

"Bye," he said.

Simone shouldered her way past Josie, who stood speechless in the doorway.

"You coming in?" he said, trying to keep the hope from his voice.

"I'm afraid to." Her eyes darted around the room.

"You just said you're done being afraid."

"I lied."

"Close the damn door, Jo."

She did but remained near the door. For a quick escape, maybe?

"I don't know what to say." She ran her hand through blond waves. She looked different today, a little older, wiser.

"I'm a jerk," she said.

"Say it again."

"This isn't easy."

"Neither was waking up to find you gone."

"Yeah, well I thought I was doing the right thing."

"You'd fail the sensitivity lesson, Ms. Matthews."

She paced to his apartment window. "I went up north to think and got mad as hell. I'm nearly thirty and I've just figured out that I can't control anything: death, life, love." Her eyes locked onto his.

"Continue," he said, crossing his arms over his chest. He was liking this.

"I thought after Danny died, this would never happen again. I wouldn't let it. I was numb for years. Until I met you."

His chest tightened.

"You made me laugh harder than I've ever laughed, and you made me feel things..." She glanced away. "No matter how hard I tried to protect myself, I couldn't. I have no control, all the micromanaging, all the organizing, it's a big joke. I've got to let go. I have to trust."

She continued her pace, her hands fisted by her sides.

"Come here, you're making me dizzy," he said.

She took a few steps toward him, but not close enough.

"A few more, sweetheart. I'm not going to bite. Unless you want me to."

She blushed and took a step closer.

"That's my girl." He reached out his hand. When her fingers slipped into his palm his insides warmed. He coaxed her toward him and she knelt on the floor by his side.

"When the Wallace kid hit me with the car, all I could think was 'Jo will never know how I feel about her.' Then I woke up and you weren't there. I was torn up inside."

"Brett—"

"Let me finish." He kissed her hand. "I've been chasing a mirage, Jo. I thought if I did all the right things and found the right woman, my life would be perfect. I chased that mirage because deep down I was afraid to get close because I saw what my parents went through. Here I've been scared to death of sharing my feelings, then I find myself sharing them with you easily…and it feels good. I guess what I'm trying to say is, you're the biggest surprise of my life, Josie Matthews. You've been right here, all this time, and I never even noticed. How stupid am I?"

"Not as stupid as me. I *knew* it was love and tried to run from it. How can you ever forgive me?" she said, pressing her cheek to his chest.

"Oh, I'll think of a way, don't worry."

"Pipes broken again?"

"Not those pipes."

"Brett!" She slapped his leg and he winced. "Sorry, sorry." She started to pull away.

"No, stay right here, don't go," he said.

Threading his fingers through her hair, he said, "I

know this is going to sound crazy, Jo, but I like being a cop.''

Silence.

"But I like you more," he said. "I'll quit if you want me to."

She looked into his eyes. "Don't quit for me. I'd never forgive myself. I want you to be happy."

"If we spend the rest of our lives together you'll be okay with me being a cop?"

"I love you for who you are, Brett. Haven't you figured that out by now?"

His chest burst with relief. "Yeah, I guess I have."

A few seconds passed. "Jo?"

"Yeah?"

"Do you think you'd want to?"

"What?"

"Marry me?"

"Well…" she hedged.

"What?" He panicked.

"There still is one problem."

His heart skipped. "What?"

"You haven't passed your final exam."

"Oh, that."

"Come on, Detective, you can do it."

He looked into her playful eyes and took a deep, relaxing breath. *"I love you."*

"Say it again." She winked and kissed him.

* * * * *

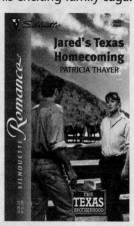

**Like a spent wave,
washing broken shells back to sea,
the clues to a long-ago death had been
caught in the undertow of time...**

Coming in
July 2003

Undertow

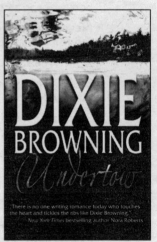

Cold cases were
Gray Hollowell's specialty,
and for a bored detective
on disability, turning over
clues from a twenty-seven-
year-old boating fatality
on exclusive Henry Island
was just the vacation he
needed. Edgar Henry had
paid him cash, given him
the keys to his cottage, told him what he knew about
his wife's death—then up and died. But it wasn't until
Edgar's vulnerable daughter, Mariah, showed up to
scatter Edgar's ashes that Gray felt the pull of her
innocent beauty—and the chill of this cold case.

Only from Silhouette Books!

COMING NEXT MONTH

#1678 BEAUTY & THE BEASTLY RANCHER—
Judy Christenberry
From the Circle K
Anna Pointer agreed to a marriage of convenience for the sake of her
kids. After all, Joe Crawford was kind, generous—her children loved
him—and he was handsome, too! But Joe thought he could only offer
his money and his name. Could Anna convince her husband that he was
her Prince Charming?

#1679 DISTRACTING DAD—Terry Essig
Nothing encourages romance like…*a flood?* When Nate Parker's dad
accidentally flooded Allie MacLord's apartment, Nate let his beautiful
neighbor bunk with him—but he had no intention of falling in love.
But then neighborly affection included Allie's sweet kisses….

#1680 JARED'S TEXAS HOMECOMING—
Patricia Thayer
The Texas Brotherhood
Jared Trager went to Texas to find his deceased brother's son—and
became a stepfather to the boy! Dana Shayne thought Jared was a
guardian angel sent to save her farm and her heart. But could she forgive his deceit when she learned his true intentions?

#1681 DID YOU SAY…*WIFE?*—Judith McWilliams
Secretary Joselyn Stemic was secretly in love with
Lucas Tarrington—her sexy boss! So when an accident left Lucas
with amnesia, she pretended to be his wife. At first it was just so the
hospital would let her care for him—but what would happen when she
took her "husband" home?

#1682 MARRIED IN A MONTH—Linda Goodnight
Love-shy rancher Colt Garret didn't know a thing about babies and
never wanted a wife. Then he received custody of a two-month-old
and desperately turned to Kati Winslow for help. Kati agreed to be
the nanny for baby Evan…if Colt agreed to marry her in a month!

#1683 DAD TODAY, GROOM TOMORROW—Holly Jacobs
Perry Square
Louisa Clancy had left home eight years ago with a big check
and an even bigger secret. She'd thought she put the past behind
her—then Joe Delacamp came into her store and spotted *their* son.
Was this long-lost love about to threaten all Louisa's dreams? Or
would it fulfill her deepest longings…?

SRCNM0703